FOLLOWING ON

RAY HOBBS

Wingspan Press

Copyright © 2016 by Ray Hobbs

All rights reserved.

This book is a work of fiction. Names, characters, settings and incidents are either the product of the author's imagination or used fictitiously. Any resemblance to actual events, settings or persons, living or dead, is entirely coincidental.

No part of this book may be reproduced or transmitted in any form or by any means, electronic or mechanical, including photocopying, recording or by any information storage and retrieval system, without written permission from the author, except for the inclusion of brief quotations in reviews.

Published in the United States and the United Kingdom
by WingSpan Press, Livermore, CA

The WingSpan name, logo and colophon are the trademarks of WingSpan Publishing.

ISBN 978-1-59594-584-6 (pbk.)
ISBN 978-1-59594-910-3 (ebk.)

First edition 2016

Printed in the United States of America

www.wingspanpress.com

Library of Congress Control Number 2016939287

1 2 3 4 5 6 7 8 9 10

Acknowledgements

I am grateful to my wife Sheila for tolerating my long absences and for answering seemingly random questions about hairstyle, clothing and other feminine matters that would otherwise have remained a mystery to me.

I am also indebted to my brother Chris, who acted as soundboard as well as a ready source of ideas during the planning, writing and revision of this book.

RH

Author's Note

The story of the New Albion Dance Orchestra, referred to in Chapter 36, is told in *Second Wind* by Ray Hobbs, published by Spiderwize.

RH

Glossary for Readers outside the UK

Grammar school:	a selective school for ages 11-18, now largely superseded by the all-ability comprehensive school
Forms 2, 3 and 5 (until 1990):	age groups 12-13, 13-14 and 15-16 (now known as Years 8, 9 and 11)
Bill and Ben (The Flowerpot Men):	marionettes who spoke a private, incomprehensible language
Pavement:	sidewalk
Territorial (Army):	a part-time reserve
Biscuit:	cookie
GP:	general (medical) practitioner
VAD (Voluntary Aid Detachment):	an organisation of volunteer nurses who served during The Great War
Ofsted:	Office for Standards in Education
Flat:	apartment
Farthing:	one quarter of an old penny
Crammer:	provider of intensive tuition
Sandhurst:	The Royal Military Academy
(funfair) Merry-go-round:	carousel
(Field-Marshall Sir Douglas, later the Earl,) Haig:	Commander-in-Chief of the British Army on the Western Front 1915-18
(David) Lloyd George:	British Prime Minister 1916-22
A (Advanced) level:	a national examination taken in England and Wales usually at age 18
Trainers:	sneakers

1

A Pennine Village
2013

By her own assessment Plum's record as a grandparent was unexceptional. She'd observed Christmas, birthdays and minor celebrations meticulously, but the demands of work and then the series of operations that had occupied the past two years had left her with little time to spend with her family. None of it was her fault but she was nevertheless aware of a nagging sense of omission not far removed from guilt. It had troubled her increasingly through convalescence but she felt it most acutely when, having agreed to have Nicola for the school holiday, she realised how little she knew about her ten-year-old granddaughter.

Nicola's attention was currently divided between the grand piano and the recently-acquired Edwardian desk. 'You've got some big furniture,' she remarked.

Plum smiled wistfully. 'I suppose the piano is furniture now, but the desk is special. It belonged to my great-uncle.'

'Your *great*-uncle?'

'Yes, it's hard to imagine, but he was my father's uncle, and that makes him your great-great-great-uncle.' Plum stroked a lock of fair hair away from the child's eyes, enjoying the novelty. Nigel's hair was as dark as hers had been before turning increasingly grey, but the children had inherited their mother's colouring.

'When do I have to do lessons?'

'Not until tomorrow. And you won't have to work all the time.'

It was wrong that the poor child's summer holiday had to be blighted by school work. A proper granny might address the problem by baking gingerbread men or raspberry volcanoes, and despair would vanish in an ambience of cosiness and well-being. It was an appealing picture but unfortunately it wasn't a viable option for a prematurely-retired musician who barely knew a rolling pin from a pastry cutter. It was one of the personal frailties that had troubled Plum lately, so Nicola's next remark surprised her.

'I'm glad I didn't have to stay with Granny Beresford. She's far too strict.' Mrs Beresford was a proper granny, with blue-and-white storage jars, age-old recipes and the correct way to do things, but it seemed that even an accomplished matriarch could occasionally fall short of the ideal.

'You know,' said Plum, slipping her uninjured arm round Nicola's slight frame and drawing her into a hug of relief, 'I can be a bit of a dragon sometimes.'

'As if.'

'Well, you've been warned.' Speaking of grannies reminded Plum of something else that had been on her mind. 'You know,' she said, 'I'm delighted to be your gran, granny, grandma or whatever the prevailing title is, and you must never believe otherwise. I can't imagine anything better, because it's a truly wonderful thing to be. There's just one ever-so-tiny snag.' She felt Nicola brace herself, and said, 'No, it's nothing awful. You see, whilst I love being all those things, I'm not carried away with being *called* any of them. I was sixty-two earlier this month and I know you think that makes me as old as Eve, but I really don't feel old, at least until someone calls me "Gran" or "Granny", and then I feel as if I'm at least a hundred.'

'What do you want me to call you, then?'

' "Plum". That's what my friends call me.'

'Why do they call you that?'

'Because my name's Victoria. It's a variety of plum.'

'Is it?' Nicola's tone was wary, as if she suspected a leg-pull.

'Yes, it's also the Latin for "victory" and the name of a queen, but as far as we're concerned and just for the moment it's a classic red plum.'

'What other names have you got?'

'Well, I was christened "Victoria Jane". I had no say in the matter, being only a few months old at the time, or I might have held out for something grander, such as "Leonora" or "Ariadne".'

'As if.' It was apparently Nicola's favourite challenge.

'All right, but I've used several names. I'm Victoria Harvey now and I was Victoria Walsh at one time, as you know, but until the accident I worked as Victoria Linthwaite. It was my maiden name.' She detached herself from Nicola and stood up to search a shelf of CDs. 'I don't usually hang on to these things but I may have the odd one to show you. Yes, here's one,' she said, taking it from the shelf. ' "Victoria Linthwaite. A Chopin Recital",' she read, 'but I was still "Plum" to my friends.' She handed it to Nicola, who examined the photograph closely.

'When did you do this?'

'About twenty-five years ago, I think. Yes, I'd be in my late thirties when I recorded that.'

'You were still pretty, though.'

'Thank you, Nicola. I'm sure you meant that as a compliment.'

Without warning a man's voice came from the kitchen. 'Who's handing out compliments? I could use a few.'

'Come through, Paul,' said Plum. We're in the sitting room.'

The man who came into the room wore a cotton shirt and jeans that bore evidence of use in the garden but he still gave an impression of smartness. His short, grey hair skirted a crown that was tanned, like his face and arms, to the colour of mahogany, and wrinkles radiated from the corners of his eyes. 'The door was open,' he said, 'so I accepted the invitation.'

'Quite right,' said Plum, 'and it's going to stay open for as long as this hot weather lasts. Come and meet my granddaughter Nicola. Nicola, this is Mr Watson, who lives next door.'

'Hello, Nicola,' he said, enclosing her small hand between his. 'Plum told me you were coming. She said you'd have a heavy suitcase, and I'd better deal with that before I have the cup of tea I hope she's about to offer me.' He took the car key from Plum.

'He's ever so good about this sort of thing,' said Plum when he was out of the room. 'He helps me with all the wretched jobs that need two hands.' Then, mindful not to inflict her frustration on Nicola, she said, 'I'd better make some fresh tea.'

'Can I do it, Gran— Plum?'

'Of course. Do you know where everything is?'

'I think so.' She got up and took the teapot to the kitchen just as Paul returned with her suitcase.

'Where would you like it?'

'First right off the landing,' Plum told him, feeling quite spare as she was the only one doing nothing. She decided to see if Nicola needed help but found when she reached the kitchen that her granddaughter had everything in hand. She was very competent in spite of her parents' worries.

Plum carried the teapot into the sitting room and said, 'Thanks for doing that, Nicola. Now, would you like to go upstairs and unpack? There are hangers in the wardrobe and the drawers are all empty. I'd like to have a word with Mr Watson while you do that.'

Paul took the armchair opposite Plum and accepted a cup of tea.

'Nicola's struggling at school,' said Plum when her granddaughter was out of earshot, 'and rather than give the poor little scrap the rest she needs, her parents have sent her to me for holiday coaching in the three "R"s while she helps me around the house.'

'But presumably you agreed to it.'

'Only because I'd rather she came here than went anywhere else. At least I can ration the work and give her a few treats. I really don't see why the poor child should suffer because her parents find her school report embarrassing.'

'There's no future in struggling at school,' said Paul confidently. 'I did as little work as possible and it never held me back.'

Plum smiled indulgently. 'It sounds like a formula for a life of contentment. What did you do when you left school?'

'I spent two years assembling prefabricated garages and then I joined the Navy. That's how I learned my trade.'

'Really?' Paul was a photographer and it seemed an odd combination. 'You must tell me about it some time. Actually,' she said as she was reminded of something else, 'you may be able to tell me something about this.' She took a small, buff envelope from the desk and handed it to him.

' "Major H.F. Linthwaite, D.S.O., M.C. and Bar",' he read. 'A relative of yours?'

'My great-uncle. Apparently the DSO is the Distinguished Service Order and the MC is the Military Cross. It's the "bar" that's been puzzling me. I'm sure the answer's out there on the internet, but you know what I'm like with computers.'

'It means he was awarded it twice. Instead of giving them another medal they gave them a bar to wear on the existing ribbon.' He examined the worn envelope. 'I imagine he was in the First World War.'

'That's right. Come and look at this.' She took him over to the desk and pulled out a drawer that might at one time have held stamps and maybe sealing wax and paper clips. Then, with the drawer fully out, she pressed on one of the side panels of the recess and it swivelled to expose a voluminous hidden compartment. 'I found it quite by accident,' she told him, 'and the envelope was inside with a lot of other letters and things.'

'He must have been quite a hoarder.'

She shrugged. 'He may just have kept those that were important to him. It would make sense in those days when letter-writing was more common.'

'Common enough to require a desk of substance,' he said, stroking its mahogany side. 'You haven't had this long, have you?'

'Only a few days. It was my uncle's. He died recently, and my cousin couldn't wait to get rid of it. The secret compartment came as a complete surprise to her.'

'Right, so was Major Linthwaite your uncle's father?'

'No, he had no children, which was possibly a shame.' She motioned to him to sit down again. 'For some reason the family saw him as something of a black sheep. I only met him a few times, the first time at my father's funeral, and I found him charming. He said I made him think of the daughter he never had. The rest of the family were very uneasy about him, though, and it created a bit of an atmosphere, not that he seemed to mind. At the time I was waiting to hear if I'd won a scholarship to the Royal College of Music, and we rather hit it off because he was a pianist too. He left me his piano in his will.'

'This one?'

'Yes. I was lucky, because he left the instruction for the rest of his estate to be sold by auction and the proceeds invested as a bursary for music students. That's how my uncle came by the desk, by the way.'

He let her refill his cup. 'You evidently made quite an impression on him.'

'Yes, my father had been very ill for some time, and his death rather came as a relief, so his funeral wasn't the ordeal for us that it might have been. Certain members of the family tried to create one – they were adept at that – but Great-Uncle Hugh was different. He was dignified and respectful, but charming as well, and I really warmed to him.'

'And he left you his Steinway.'

'Yes.' She smiled, remembering something else. 'He told me a story about a piano he'd bought shortly after the Great War. It was quite a modest upright piano but even in old age he spoke of it with great affection. It was important to him at a very difficult time.'

2

A West Riding Town
1920

After his army medical board in 1918 Hugh Linthwaite vowed privately to avoid responsibility and decision-making for the rest of his life. It was an impulsive gesture, a reaction born of the immediate sense of finality that came with his discharge, and he soon realised the resolution would be impossible to keep. All the same, his purchase of a new upright piano came only after two years' dogged procrastination.

Its case was finished in black, and that appealed to Hugh. He found the ever-popular walnut fussy. Also, its lines were clean; the mouldings that framed the three rectangular front panels were simple and pleasing, but even more important was the absence of sconces. Candles reminded him of trenches and dugouts.

He lifted the fall to reveal the manufacturer's name: Friedrich Marschner of Dresden.

'They're a small firm,' Mr Gledhill told him, 'but they've been making pianos since the end of the last century. Let me make more space and I'll get you a stool.' He pushed the piano back, dismissing Hugh's offer of help. 'No, leave it to me,' he insisted. 'I do this all the time.'

At twenty-eight Hugh found it galling to be regarded as helpless but he could have offered little assistance, dependent as he was on his walking stick.

'There you are.' Like a dignitary unveiling a plaque, Mr Gledhill placed the stool in front of the piano and stood back to let Hugh in. 'See what you think.'

Hugh played a few exploratory scales and was captivated at once by the richness of the tone.

'What do you think of it, Mr Linthwaite?' The proprietor perched on a nearby stool to listen.

'It's remarkable.' He played a few isolated chords and said, 'There's something quite unique about it, a special kind of warmth.'

'What about the action?'

'It's perfectly weighted; at least it seems to be. I confess I've no real knowledge of that side of things but it certainly feels right.'

'Why don't you try it with something more testing than scales?' Mr Gledhill was always happy for Hugh to try his pianos. He had long since abandoned any expectation of selling him one, but a pianist of Hugh's quality attracted customers to the shop, and his services were free. He was a frequent visitor as well, so that shoppers had come to associate him with the piano department and looked out for him when they called in from Saturday shopping. Some knew him because he taught music at the grammar school; to others he was the slight young man with prematurely-greying hair, who was happy to provide an enjoyable musical interlude on a rainy afternoon.

On this occasion, however, his attention was concentrated on the instrument itself and, partly in response to Mr Gledhill's suggestion but largely out of curiosity, he tried the opening of an intermezzo by Brahms. He had intended to play only a few bars, but the feel of the piano and its tone were so compelling that he played to the end. It was self-indulgence of a kind he'd almost forgotten and it wasn't long before he and Mr Gledhill were discussing delivery.

* * *

He arrived at Cullington Grammar School on the following Monday morning and had just opened the door to the common room when Baxter, the Senior Master, spotted him.

'Good morning, Linthwaite,' he said. 'Colonel Pickford wants to see you in his study before assembly.'

'Does he really?' Hugh glanced at the clock on the mantelpiece. His knee was troubling him and he had been planning to rest it for a few minutes.

'I'd go now,' said Baxter. 'Don't keep him waiting.'

Dutifully Hugh straightened his gown and adjusted his tie. Pickford liked his staff to be smartly turned out. He also liked them to be punctual, and was drumming with his fingers on his desk when Hugh arrived.

'You took your time getting here, Linthwaite.' He eyed Hugh crossly and his moustache trembled as if it were independent of the fleshy, humourless face to which it belonged.

'I came as soon as Baxter told me you wanted to see me, Headmaster.'

'Why on earth must you twitch that way?'

'It's my knee. It's particularly painful this morning.'

'Oh well, I shan't keep you long. I want to check that the arrangements for Founder's Day and Prize-Giving are in place. The third of November's not far away. I take it you've got the choir and the orchestra bashed into shape?'

'Yes, Headmaster.'

Pickford's resentment at that form of address was a source of sly amusement for the dissident minority on his staff. He had served in a reserve battalion in England throughout the war but still expected to be addressed by his wartime rank, an affectation that Hugh was determined not to encourage.

'What's the choir going to sing?'

'A chorus from Schubert's *Mass in G* and one from Haydn's *The Creation*.'

'German music?'

'The composers were both Austrian, Headmaster. The Schubert will be sung in Latin and the Haydn in English, if that helps.'

'I see. Well, that's something, I suppose. Tuneful, are they, these items?'

'Fairly bursting with tunes.'

'And the concert items for Prize-Giving?'

'They are equally tuneful, Headmaster.' He wished Pickford would end the inquisition and let him go. The pain in his knee was worse than ever.

'I meant, are they ready?' A man of scant humour, Pickford disliked levity.

'They're all in hand.'

'Is that girl in the fifth form going to play the violin?'

'Rose Balmforth? Yes, she'll be taking part.' It was typical of Pickford to insist on including Rose in the concert. She had private lessons, so the school could take no credit for her playing, but it seemed the man had no conscience.

'Good, I'll look forward to that.' Pickford made a backhand gesture of dismissal and then looked up again a few seconds later to find Hugh still present. 'Well,' he demanded, 'what is it?'

'I have a letter from the military hospital, Headmaster.' Hugh took the letter from his inside pocket and handed it to Pickford. 'They want to see me next Tuesday for my disability pension review.'

Pickford only glanced at the letter and handed it back to him. 'Well, if you must go, you must. Ask Baxter to arrange cover for your lessons.'

The tone of the meeting was all that Hugh had come to expect, but he was able to dismiss it from his mind as the rest of his day was infinitely pleasanter, consisting of Music with 3A and 3B girls, then 3A and 3B boys, 2A and 2B girls followed by the boys of that year, and English with 3A girls. At choir practice during the lunch interval the sexes were separated only by the voices nature had given them, an altogether civilised way to make music. The highlight of the day, however, was his rehearsal with Rose Balmforth for the Prize-Giving concert.

She was waiting for him with her music stand already set up in the hall when he arrived. She handed him the piano part of Mozart's Sixth Sonata.

'Thank you, Rose. It's the first movement, isn't it?'

'Yes, sir.' She was a small child with light auburn hair, delicate features and, by contrast, a strong local accent.

'I see.' He scanned the first three pages and said, 'Do you mind if I take this home and do some work on it?'

'No, it'll be all right, sir. Miss Bainbridge can't really play it. She isn't right good on the piano.'

He smiled at her frankness. 'We can't be good at everything, Rose, and I imagine she plays the violin beautifully.'

'Oh yes, sir, she does.'

'You should hear me play the violin.'

The remark clearly took Rose by surprise. 'I didn't know you played, sir.'

'I took it up as a boy but I was so awful my violin teacher went to live in New Zealand.'

Recognising a leg-pull, she smiled and said, 'You can't have been that bad, sir.'

'No, I was even worse than that, but it just demonstrates that we all have our strengths and weaknesses, and your strength is playing the fiddle, so let's make a start, shall we?'

She tuned to his 'A', and then turned to him with a smiling nod and they started the movement. It was unfamiliar to him but he was a capable sight-reader and he was able to enjoy the experience. It seemed incredible that a fifteen-year-old child could be so talented. Her playing was sheer joy, and he wondered for a moment if all his pleasures were arriving together. If they were, they were long overdue but no less welcome.

3

'I wish they were all as easy as the five-times table.'

'I know, Nicola, but wishing doesn't make anything happen. I still think the best way is to learn them by heart. Do you like singing?' It was a beautiful, sunny morning and Plum intended to spend some time in the garden before lunch, but the six-times table had to come first.

'Yes, I like it when we do singing at school.'

'All right.' Plum experimented for a minute on the piano with her right hand, and said, 'Sing after me: two sixes are twelve, three sixes are eighteen.'

Nicola repeated the line. She had a pleasant voice.

'Again, with me.' They repeated the line. 'Now for the next three: four sixes are twenty-four, five sixes are thirty, six sixes are thirty-six.' They repeated it twice. 'Now from the beginning and you've learned half of it already.' They did that three times and as far as Plum was concerned half was enough for the time being; the rest could wait. 'Let's go into the garden.'

'What are we going to do?'

'We're going to pick some peas before the birds make off with them. With some carrots I've got, they'll go nicely with cottage pie.'

'Is that what we're having?' The prospect evidently appealed to Nicola

'Tonight, yes.'

'What are we having for lunch?'

'I haven't decided yet. You mustn't expect organisation from me, but I'll think of something, and then after lunch we're going to try some baking. It's time I behaved like a proper granny.'

'Do you have to?'

'Why shouldn't I?'

''Cause you're twice as better as you are.'

'I could be twice as good or I could be better, but not "twice as better," Nicola. Either way, I think you're being far too kind. I could struggle to live up to your expectations.'

'Most grannies can't do times tables on the piano.'

'On the piano,' Plum conceded, 'I do have an advantage over the conventional granny, even with one hand. It's the other bits I need to work on.'

Nicola changed the subject abruptly. 'Plum,' she asked, 'what was Granddad like? I didn't know him a lot.'

'You mean you didn't know him *well*. You're talking about Granddad Harvey, I imagine.'

'Yes.'

'Well, how do you remember him?'

'He was nice.'

'That's right.' Plum swung her legs over the piano stool to sit facing her. 'He was kind, honest and generous; in fact he was lovely. It's a shame you didn't see more of him.'

'It was a shame about the accident.'

'Yes.' Plum studied her feet briefly. 'I can't disagree with that.'

'He wasn't my real granddad though, was he?'

'No.'

'What was Granddad Walsh like?'

'Oh, let me see.' She tried to think of a diplomatic description. 'He was very clever. I do remember that, and he was popular as well.'

'So why did you get divorced?'

Thinking quickly, Plum said, 'You know how you can be special friends with someone, and then something happens and you break friends with them?'

'Yes.'

'That's what happened. I broke friends with him and he went away.' She stood up and said, 'Let's go into the garden. We can talk out there.' She picked up a bottle of sun-screen, hoping the change of scene might provide a distraction and a change of subject.

Nicola proved adept at finding peapods but was still full of questions. She asked, 'What are these CDs hanging up on strings for?'

'They're to scare the birds away. They flash in the sunlight and startle them. At least, that's the theory.' She examined one and said, 'You'd think the Brahms B flat Concerto would do the trick. It's terrified enough pianists in its time.'

They continued picking until Plum considered they had enough. 'We can shell them out here,' she said. 'Drop the peas in the saucepan and the pods can go straight into the compost bin.'

'Have you always been good at gardening?'

Plum laughed good-naturedly. 'Darling, if I'm good at gardening, Bill and Ben should teach elocution. I inherited this lot when I bought the house three months ago. Even if we'd had a garden in London, I doubt if I'd ever have found time to do anything in it.' Watching Nicola open a pod and empty it deftly into the saucepan, she remarked, 'You've shelled peas before.'

'Mm, we have a garden at school.'

'What a good idea. Did it say anything about gardening in your school report?'

'No, it was all about reading and writing and maths, the things I can't do.' After a moment's thought, she said, 'It's like you. You talk all the time about what you can't do, like baking and gardening. You never say anything about the things you're good at.'

It was a fair point and it was perhaps time for a serious conversation. 'Maybe it's not good to say too much about the things we do well, Nicola. It would never do for people to get the wrong idea and think we're boasting.'

'No, it wouldn't.'

'On the other hand, you've got a point. I probably think rather too much about the things I don't do well, mainly because I can no longer do the one thing I did particularly well. Do you follow me?'

'Do you mean playing the piano?'

'That's right. It was all so sudden, you see. One minute I was happily married and doing the thing I loved best and the next I knew I'd lost both those things. I used to practise for at least five hours every day, and now I have to improve each of those shining hours with other activities. That and learning to live alone are not easy things to do.'

Nicola merely nodded and continued to shell peas, but it was evident from her preoccupied frown that she was thinking about what Plum had said.

'You worry about the things you find difficult, ' said Plum, 'but you also have qualities, excellent ones that are much more important than multiplication tables and spelling, and it's wise to remember that.' She moved the saucepan aside as if it represented a barrier between them. 'We should both work on the things we need to improve, but I agree we should take stock and remember our good points as well.'

Nicola picked uncertainly at an empty peapod. 'It's hard.'

'What's hard? Do you mean you can't think of any good points?'

She nodded uncertainly.

'Let me get you started.' A wasp had settled on the handle of the saucepan and Plum wafted it away. It was no time for distractions. 'Three things I've learned about you already,' she said, 'are that you're caring, you're capable and you're honest. They're all very important qualities and I'm sure I'll discover more very soon.'

'Do you mean it?'

'I mean every word.'

That seemed to please Nicola. After a moment she said, 'It's your turn now.'

'My turn to think of things I'm good at?' Plum thought for a while and said, 'I think we're both too modest, Nicola, because I can't think of anything either.'

'I can.' She sounded unusually confident.

'Fire away, I'm listening.'

'Okay. You're kind.'

'Thank you.'

'And other grannies don't look as nice as you. You've got a nice figure and you're really nice-looking.'

'You lovely child. Come here.' Plum swept her up and hugged her. 'You can come and stay with me again and again and again. Just keep the compliments flowing.'

'That's not the most important thing though.' Nicola detached herself so that she could make her point. 'You're like a friend.'

'That's a big compliment. Thank you.'

'To be proper friends we have to say, "Make Friends, Make Friends." Do you know it?'

'I don't think so.'

'Okay, give me your little finger and I'll say it first. Then we have to say it together like we did with the times tables.'

'Right.' Plum hooked the little finger of her right hand around Nicola's, wondering what to expect.

'Ready?'

'Ready.'

Nicola took a breath and began. ' "Make friends, make friends, never, never break friends. If you do I'll flush you down the loo and that will be the end of you!" '

Plum participated in the reprise and considered herself thoroughly befriended. It was difficult to know what to say next, but a voice from over the fence saved her.

'Hello.'

'Good morning, Paul.'

'I come with an RPC.'

'What on earth is an RPC?' Plum wondered if it might be another esoteric ceremony.

'A Request for the Pleasure of your Company,' he translated. 'I'd like to invite you ladies to lunch at my place today. I've been stood up.'

'We'd love to come. Thank you, Paul.' Turning to Nicola, she said, 'There, I told you lunch would happen.'

'But that's cheating.'

'It'll be better than anything I might have rustled up. What are we eating, Paul?'

'Home-made turkey burgers with associated bits and pieces, and I've prepared a tossed salad to ease the conscience. My daughter and her children were coming but my grandson Henry fell off the garden wall this morning and broke his arm. The poor little bloke's at Cullington General now, being plastered up.'

'That's awful. How old is he?'

'Six. He's the youngest.'

'I broke my arm when I was six,' Nicola told him.

'That's handy. You'll be able to give him lots of advice when you meet.'

'Mm.' It was apparent that her thoughts had moved on. 'I've never had a turkey burger,' she said.

'You're in for a treat,' said Plum. 'When Mr Watson says "home-made", you jump in quickly. He's a granddad who knows his way around a kitchen.'

'Come over now,' said Paul. 'The sun's over the satellite dish, so we can have a drink while I flash up the barbie.'

They sat beneath a large awning while Paul poured a glass of white Bordeaux for Plum and orange juice for Nicola. 'I've been thinking about that great-uncle of yours,' he said. 'A major with awards for gallantry must have seen a lot of action. My granddad was on the Western Front from nineteen-sixteen and he hardly ever spoke of it. From the little he said, though, it sounded like hell on earth.'

'Uncle Hugh hardly referred to it but he did say that for some time after the war he slept badly. I believe he was unhappy at work as well, and that can't have helped. He enjoyed teaching, but the regime at Cullington Grammar School was far from pleasant.'

4

Hugh returned from his review at the hospital to find that he was to cover a games lesson with 3A and 3B for 'Bruiser' Barnes, who was suffering concussion after tripping over his own bootlace and colliding with an earthenware sink. The boys had given the accident-prone Barnes his nickname and were still laughing about the incident when Hugh arrived at the changing room.

'Calm down now, boys.' He was in a good mood, having enjoyed a rare night of uninterrupted sleep. He waited a few moments until they were silent, and then called for excuse notes. Three boys obliged him.

'Thank you, Palmer, Longbottom and Andrews. Let's see what you're suffering from this week.' He opened the notes in turn. 'Ah, Palmer, I see you've convinced your mother that you've twisted your ankle, although it seems robust enough to me. And Andrews, your mother believes you've pulled a muscle in your side. Oh dear, oh dear.' He held up the third note with theatrical disbelief and said, 'Longbottom, how on earth did you convince your unfortunate, gullible parent of this?' He folded the note reverently and placed it in his hip pocket with the others. 'I see a future for you, my lad, either in the law or in politics. You could achieve notoriety in either calling.' Raising his voice, he called, 'Into your kit, boys, as quick as you like.'

They changed and followed him to the football field. The three who had brought excuse notes walked beside him.

Longbottom asked, 'Sir, what's that thing you're carrying?'
'It's a shooting stick, Longbottom.'
The boy seemed puzzled. 'But sir, surely you can't shoot with it.'
'No, it's not a gun. If it were, don't you think I'd have shot you before now? I've been tempted, you know.'
'So is it for resting your gun on when you're shooting, sir?'
'No, Longbottom, it's a portable seat that I use when I'm taking a games period. It saves my knee.'
'Ah, I see, sir.'
Andrews asked, 'Sir, is it true, sir, that Mr Barnes had the job of flogging deserters in the war, sir?'
Hugh suspected that the question was less than ingenuous. 'I doubt it very strongly, Andrews.'
'Because, I mean, sir, that's what everybody says, sir.'
'In that case they should stop talking nonsense.'
'That's what I say, sir.'
'I'm glad to hear it, Andrews.'
When they were assembled beside the football pitch Hugh counted thirteen from 3A and twelve from 3B, so he let the form captains go ahead and pick their teams. When they had done that, he wasn't surprised to find that the remaining three were the least athletic boys in the year. He made two of them linesmen and that left Hoyle, a boy of generous proportions and with shorts that reached almost to his ankles.
'Hoyle,' he said, 'Go downhill and stand behind the goal net where it's torn.'
'Yes, sir.'
'And if the ball goes through the hole in the net I want you to stop it before it goes any further. If Wilkinson asks you what you're doing behind his net you can tell him I've put you in charge of the perimeter.'
'Yes, sir.' With his sudden and unexpected responsibility Hoyle went happily on his way. Hugh leaned on his shooting stick and called, 'Play!'
He was easing his weight away from his right knee when he heard Palmer whisper urgently to the others. Hearing the nickname 'Mary', he followed Palmer's gaze and saw Pickford making his way towards them. At that point, the game suddenly reclaimed his attention.
'Stop! I saw that, Hartley.'

'It was an accident, sir.'

'It may well have been but it's still a free kick to Three A. Take the kick from the half-way line, Porter.'

3A's captain was taking the free kick as Pickford arrived at Hugh's side.

'Good afternoon, Linthwaite.'

'Good afternoon, Headmaster.'

Pickford waited pointedly whilst Hugh struggled to his feet. The three boys were already heading tactfully towards the perimeter track.

'I see you still haven't invested in a whistle. I seem to remember we had this conversation earlier.'

'I remember it too, Headmaster.'

'Then how the devil do you expect to referee a football match without one?'

'It's not difficult. The boys can hear me well enough.' As if to demonstrate, he broke off to bellow over Pickford's shoulder, 'Get rid of it, Hartley!'

Pickford winced. 'Have it your own way if you feel you must. I actually came to ask you if everything is ready for tomorrow evening.'

Hugh struggled to control his twitch. It was possibly the fifth time Pickford had quizzed him about Founder's Day and Prize-Giving. 'Everything is in place,' he said.

'Good. I know you've got this operation on your mind but I don't want any slip-ups. You're far too easy-going, Linthwaite.'

Hugh rested gratefully on his shooting stick as Pickford receded. The whistle business had just been another opportunity for a browbeating. Like many other infantry officers, Hugh had discarded his whistle at the end of the war and had no intention of using one again. Whether or not Pickford understood the reason for his refusal was open to speculation but he certainly saw it as a weakness to be exploited. He was also trying to make Hugh feel guilty about going into hospital again. That had been inevitable.

'Goal, sir!' The three boys had returned and Palmer was pointing downhill to where several boys were gathered. 'I think there's an injury as well, sir, but I can't see who it is.'

Hugh levered himself upright again but two boys from 3A saved him the journey. Between them they supported Hoyle, whose bloodied nose and mouth told their own story.

'It went through t' hole in t' net and hit him full in t' face, sir,' one of the boys told him with unconcealed amusement.

'But I stopped it, sir,' Hoyle mumbled in painful triumph.

'You did well, Hoyle,' said Hugh, 'and I'm sorry you were hurt. I'm afraid responsibility usually comes at a price.'

* * *

For some reason he found the encounter with Pickford hard to dismiss from his thoughts. It was possible that the prospect of another painful operation had made him more vulnerable than usual to the man's pettiness, but whatever the reason, it returned to him several times that evening as he sat marking books, and it stayed with him well into the night. Consequently, when he arrived at school in the morning for Founder's Day and Prize-Giving he was tired and irritable.

In the event, the choir sang well, the orchestra was acceptable, and Rose's solo was all he'd expected. Unfortunately, at least for him, the evening's success was overshadowed by an innovation on Pickford's part: the general singing of 'Land of Hope and Glory', and the sight of the headmaster, pious and pompous in song, turned Hugh's irritation to anger.

He was still angry when he let himself into his house and it was a while before he could face the cold beef and pickles left for him by Mrs Naylor, his part-time housekeeper. She had lit a fire for him as well, so that he would have hot water. A note on the kitchen table informed him that she had ordered five bags of coal. If only the rest of his life were as uncomplicated.

When he had eaten, he took one of his powders and went to bed.

* * *

He knew he was dreaming. Everything about the dream was familiar, including the feeling of panic at being unable to halt it. He tried to call out to rouse himself but his jaws were clenched. Also, an unseen force was pushing him forward so that he was compelled to take step after step to remain upright, while around him men lay ominously still. Where there should be gunfire, running footsteps and the shouts and screams of men in battle there was silence and a looming and menacing sense of apprehension that grew in intensity until the ghastly moment of realisation that all eyes were open, staring at him in silent and baleful reproach.

And then he was upright, soaked in perspiration and somewhere between nightmare and reality. He was aware of the bed clothes and the ticking of the clock but the eyes were there in the room.

For what seemed an age he remained in that dreadful limbo until reason gradually asserted itself and the dream took its proper place as a memory. Even then, its images stayed with him.

After some time, he tried wiping the perspiration from his eyes with a sodden pyjama sleeve, and the cold clamminess of it roused him to full wakefulness. Still breathless, he groped around until he found the electric light switch and when his eyes had adjusted to the brightness he abandoned the saturated sheets and found his slippers, dressing gown and stick.

In consideration of Hugh's disability, one of his father's last acts had been to have a bathroom installed next to the ground floor bedroom, and for that Hugh was especially grateful. He laid coals over the glowing embers of the sitting room fire and by the time he was out of the bath they were well alight, so he dressed in his day clothes by the fireside. The clock showed ten minutes to four.

He sat for a while drinking tea as he usually did when sleep was no longer possible. Only occasionally he resorted to a glass of cognac. He'd seen too many tortured souls pay the penalty for refuge in alcohol. Besides, tea taken in a china cup and saucer epitomised those peacetime luxuries of comfort and wellbeing that were the antithesis of everything he preferred to forget.

But the images persisted despite his efforts to dispel them. They often came and went as if by some malevolent design, most often when he was overwrought, and on this occasion they were slow to recede.

He cast around for a distraction and his eye fell on the new piano. He had been so preoccupied during the past few days that he had neglected it, and now the need to play was compelling. Grasping his stick, he rose to his feet and limped across to the stool.

He sat for a few moments, touching the keys and enjoying the pale smoothness of the ivories. Then, with little conscious thought, he began the slow movement of Beethoven's *Sonata Pathétique*. The warm key of A flat was soothing, and as he played he became absorbed in the music.

5

'Are we going to get a sieve so that we don't have to borrow Mr Watson's again?'

'I've got it on my list.' Had it not been for Nicola's timely intervention, the cake would have contained lumpy flour and Plum would have been embarrassed. As it happened, the final result was quite acceptable and Paul had ungrudgingly given her eight out of ten, a good mark for a first attempt. She intended to build on her achievement, but her immediate priority was to arrange the letters from the secret compartment in chronological order. It was quite difficult because she was tempted to read them as she took them from their envelopes, and that wasted time. It had occurred to her that the exercise might be seen as an invasion of Uncle Hugh's privacy, but she excused herself with the knowledge that she was doing it out of loyalty to him and to discover the truth, so maybe it wasn't such a bad thing. And now she had made a discovery.

'What have you found, Plum?'

'A letter dated the eleventh of November, nineteen-twenty. Come and look.'

Nicola came to her side and frowned in disgust. 'It smells awful,' she said.

'Paper does smell as it gets older. You will too.'

'I hope I won't smell like that.'

'Let's hope not. This letter came from a very clean place, as well: Beckett Park Military Hospital.'

'Where's that?'

'Look, here's the address.' She was aware of Nicola's reliance on others to do her reading, and the weaning process had to begin sometime.

' "Head…" '

'Break the word up.'

' "Head…ing…ley, Leeds." '

'Good girl.'

'The letters look funny.'

Plum could see she was now looking at the text of the letter. 'Yes, it was written with a typewriter.'

'What's that?'

'It was what people used for writing business letters before everyone had a computer. It had a keyboard with letters laid out almost as they are now and when you pressed one a lever with a letter on it made of lead flew towards a sheet of paper wound around a rubber thing shaped like a rolling pin.' There was incredulity on the child's face, but she pressed on. 'Before it could reach the paper a ribbon soaked in ink jumped up in front of it, and then the lead letter smacked the ribbon against the paper and – hey presto – the letter was printed in ink on the paper.'

Nicola was shaking, her cheeks were wet and she was helpless with laughter.

'Enjoy the joke, darling. The twentieth century's full of them.' She waited for the laughter to subside, and was about to ask Nicola to read more of the letter when the phone rang. It was Nigel.

'I'm just phoning to find out if Nicola's behaving herself.'

'Are you really? In that case we'll forget about the bit where you're supposed to say, "Hello, Mum, how are you?" And I say, "I'll be all right when the ambulance arrives, but never mind that. How are you?" '

After a deep sigh Nigel said, 'You are all right, I take it?'

'Yes, thank you, Nigel. I'm actually all the better for the delightful company I'm keeping. Nicola is being very helpful and her studies are coming on apace. However, I'll let her tell you about that. I imagine you'd like to speak to her?'

'Yes, please.'

Plum handed the phone to Nicola, saying, 'I'll be in the kitchen.' As she went, she heard her granddaughter say, 'Hello, Dad, I know the six-times table now, and we're going to do the seven-times tomorrow.' Plum hoped her son would be impressed.

Nicola joined her in the kitchen after less than a minute. 'He told me I haven't to be a nuisance,' she said, looking deflated.

'Ah, then my theory is correct.'

'What do you mean?'

'He really is confusing you with someone else. I've suspected it for some time. Did you speak to your mum?'

'No, she was out.'

'Too bad.' She held out her arm to administer a hug. 'What's your favourite sticky treat?'

'Ice cream.'

That was easy. 'What flavour?'

'All of them.'

'I've none in the freezer, so let's go to the supermarket and get some.' They disentangled and went out to the car.

On the way, Nicola said, 'I like your car. It's really funny.'

'It has me rolling in the aisle too. What do you find funny about it?'

'It does things all by itself.'

'Ah, you're talking about these magic buttons.' She passed her thumb over the steering-column controls. 'Well, with me in the driving seat it has to do most of the work.'

Nicola was quiet for a while, and then she asked, 'Will you never be able to play the piano with both hands again?'

'I'm afraid not.'

That provoked another silence before she asked, 'Was Uncle Hugh good at playing the piano?'

'He was very good. I have some of his recordings.'

'Did he make CDs?'

'No, he made gramophone records.'

'Vinyl ones?'

'Eventually, but before that they had very fragile records made of shellac and then Bakelite. I have a few in good condition though, and I had them transferred on to a CD. If you like, we can listen to one when we get back.'

'Oh good. We can read the rest of that letter as well.'

Plum smiled. 'That's the spirit, Nicola. The letter from the hospital was very important to him; in fact it was a special time because I think it was about then that he met Aunt Ellen.'

6

Hugh was spared contact with Pickford for the next week or so, and with the additional benefit of several nights' undisturbed sleep he was preparing for the Christmas carol service with more enthusiasm than he'd felt for some time. He was in the same optimistic frame of mind when he visited Gledhill's Music Shop.

Being a regular visitor, he should have remembered the shallow step outside the sheet music department. He had always negotiated it carefully in the past but, pleased at having found the music he wanted, he was about to call into the piano department for a word with Mr Gledhill, when he stumbled heavily and a stabbing pain in his right knee drove all other thoughts from his mind.

Biting his lower lip, he stood for a moment, resting his weight on his left foot, before turning towards the exit. He intended to board a tramcar as quickly as possible so that he could go home to rest his knee and take something for the pain, and was limping towards the outer door when he found a young woman beside him.

'Mr Linthwaite, isn't it?' She carried a violin case, and that stimulated his memory as much as anything, because he'd seen her at school concerts. In spite of the pain he recognised Rose Balmforth's violin teacher.

'Miss Bainbridge.' He offered her his hand. 'How are you?' They exchanged the usual greetings and then she asked tentatively, 'Are you really all right, Mr Linthwaite? You don't look at all well.'

'I'm all right really, but thank you for your concern. Unfortunately I'm on my way to an appointment so I must ask you to excuse me.' He reckoned he might still catch the three-fifty tram outside the Victoria Arcade.

'Of course. I hope we'll meet again before long.'

He took his leave of her and stepped awkwardly on to the pavement outside, turning up his collar against the drizzle.

After twenty yards or so he found his progress reduced to a hobble, and then with no warning at all his knee buckled agonisingly, causing him to fall against the wall of Harrison's Coffee House. He clung for a moment to the masonry, aware that his walking stick and hat were on the pavement and therefore beyond his reach, and that his left foot was slipping away from him against the wet flagstone. He found himself sliding to the ground, and in that same moment he heard a woman's voice.

'Mr Linthwaite!' Miss Bainbridge crouched beside him. 'What is it?'

'My knee. I... I can't get up.'

'Don't worry, I'll get someone to help.' She stood upright and looked around her. Three women with shopping bags stood close by but they all looked quite elderly. Miss Bainbridge called to them. 'Will someone help, please? I need someone to help me lift him.'

One of them asked, 'What's up? Has he had a drop too much?'

'No, he hasn't. He's injured, can't you see? I need someone to help me get him indoors.'

The others shook their heads doubtfully. One turned and pointed. 'There's a bobby down t' street,' she said, 'by Metcalfe's Drapers.'

Miss Bainbridge peered urgently down the High Street and called with surprising volume, 'Constable!'

'Aye, t' bobby's your best bet,' said the woman who had pointed him out. 'We can't lift him.'

Somewhere down the street someone took up the call for the policeman and through his embarrassment and agony Hugh heard hurrying footsteps approaching. Presently, from behind him, a man's voice asked, 'What's the trouble, miss?'

'Oh, thank goodness! Constable, will you help me get this man into Harrison's? He's in awful pain.'

'What's the injury, sir?' The policeman crouched in front of him.

'It's my knee,' Hugh gasped. 'A shrapnel wound. It does this sometimes but I'll be all right if I can sit down for a spell.'

'It seems to me you need a doctor, sir.'

'No, really, there's nothing to be done. I just need to rest it.'

The policeman looked doubtful but removed his helmet and handed it to Miss Bainbridge. 'Would you mind, miss, just so that nobody mistakes it for a souvenir?' He returned his attention to Hugh and said, 'All right, sir, hold on tight.' Hugh felt himself being borne upwards until he was able to put his good foot to the ground.

'Now, miss,' said the constable, 'if you'd like to organise a chair for the gentleman I'll help him inside. Put your arm round my shoulder, sir, and rest your weight on me.' With some difficulty they negotiated the revolving door.

Miss Bainbridge entered behind them and summoned a waitress. 'I need a chair for this man,' she said, 'and a table, please.' The waitress stared for a second and then reacted. 'Yes, miss. This one's free.' She indicated a table by the wall and pulled out a chair.

'Where did you come by this injury, sir, if you don't mind my asking?' The policeman lowered Hugh gently on to the chair.

'It's a souvenir from Messines Ridge.' Hugh leant against the back of the chair and looked up gratefully. 'Thank you, Constable. I'm very grateful to you.'

'Think nothing of it, sir. The Fourteenth, was it?'

'Yes.'

'Eleventh Battalion?'

Hugh nodded weakly.

'I thought so when you said Messines Ridge. I was in the Eighth Battalion myself, being a Leeds man.'

'You fellows have a lot to be proud of.'

'It's very civil of you to say so, sir, but I'm glad it's over all the same, as I've no doubt you are.' The policeman stood upright, straightening his tunic. 'If you're sure there's nothing more I can do, I'll be on my way. Good day, sir. Good day, miss.'

They both repeated their thanks and Miss Bainbridge took a seat across the table from Hugh, who said, 'I must thank you as well, Miss Bainbridge. I'm afraid I'm an awful nuisance.'

'You're not a nuisance at all. How's your knee?'

'Still painful but it'll wear off. I'm going into hospital soon, for an operation, hopefully the last.' The sound of a tram outside made him look around for a clock. 'I should catch the four-fifteen,' he said.

'You can't go home by tram, Mr Linthwaite. Where do you live?'

'Greenacre Road, just below the park.'

'I live not far from you. Wouldn't it be more comfortable for you, and more sensible altogether, if we took a taxicab?'

'It would, I agree.' Now that the pain was beginning to recede and he was able to think more clearly it did seem the obvious thing to do.

'I'm glad, and I think tea is also a good idea.' She caught the eye of a waitress and asked Hugh, 'Have you any preference or shall we have the house blend?'

'The house blend will be perfect, but you must let me do the honours.'

'That's very kind of you.'

He wondered a little about a violin teacher who seemed so much at home in a fashionable coffee house. Her clothes, too, had the appearance of quality, not that Hugh had any real knowledge of such things.

He ordered a pot of tea for two, and when the waitress was gone, Miss Bainbridge said, 'I've seen you quite often in Gledhill's.'

Now he thought about it, he'd seen her there too, and it was remarkable how distracting constant pain could be, because in normal circumstances he would surely have taken more notice of her. 'I bought a piano there quite recently,' he told her.

Her blue eyes widened with interest. 'Did you really? Do tell me about it.'

'It's a Marschner, a name I've never heard before, but it has an amazing tone, especially for an upright.'

'What a piece of luck to find it, but you're an excellent pianist and you need a fine instrument.'

'It's kind of you to say so.'

She waited until the waitress had set the tea things on the table, and then said to him, 'I hope you don't mind my asking, but if they've operated on your knee before, why do they need to do it again?'

'It's quite badly damaged and they keep finding tiny pieces of shrapnel and grit. They don't show up well on X-rays, but that doesn't make them less of a nuisance. They move around and get up to all kinds of mischief.'

'I see.' She lifted the teapot lid and peered inside before pouring. 'How awful it is that it's still troubling you after all this time.'

'Oh well,' he shrugged with a faint smile, "Into each life some rain must fall".'

She also smiled, recognising the line, and asked, 'Are you fond of Longfellow?'

'I'm a devotee.'

'Oh, good, he's one of my favourites too. I love *The Day is Done*, but I expect you know lots of his poems. Rose told me you teach English as well as music.'

He wondered for a moment if Rose Balmforth talked as much about him as she did about Miss Bainbridge. He was inclined to doubt it. 'I teach some English, it's true,' he said, 'but it's not really my subject.'

'Ah well, you enjoy Longfellow, and that's the main thing, although I'm sorry that some of your days are "dark and dreary".'

'They're not so dark,' he told her. 'Believe me, many men are worse off.'

'I know that, but it sounds bad enough to me. How's your knee now, by the way?'

'Much better, thank you, and I have to say it's thanks largely to you, Miss Bainbridge.'

'Not at all. Milk or lemon?'

'Milk, please, but no sugar.'

She handed him his tea. 'Don't you think,' she said, 'considering all that's happened this afternoon, that it would be a good idea to dispense with formality? I'd be pleased if you'd call me Ellen.'

'Then I shall, and my name's Hugh.' The development pleased him, just as he was pleased that she was called Ellen. The name seemed right for her.

'I hope you don't mind my asking,' she said, 'but when will your operation be? It seems rather urgent.'

'The letter came from Beckett Park only yesterday. They want me to go in on the tenth.'

'That's very short notice, isn't it?'

He smiled. 'Mr Pickford finds it very inconvenient, but I just want to get it out of the way. I live alone, so it doesn't affect anyone else.'

'I see.' She appeared to be weighing something up in her mind. 'Beckett Park Hospital is the one in Leeds, isn't it?'

'It's the military hospital in Headingley.'

'Of course. Look, I'm sure your stay will be as comfortable as they can make it, and I hope I'm not being presumptuous, but I'm told it's always good to receive letters when you're in hospital. Would you like me to write to you?'

7

With Nicola happily off to bed, Plum walked round the garden enjoying the peace and fresh air. As she moved nearer the fence she found Paul doing the same. It occurred to her then that she hadn't seen him since early afternoon, so she asked, 'How's Henry?'

'Hello Plum. He's all right now; in fact he's quite proud of his plaster cast.'

'I expect it'll give him a degree of *cachet* with his friends.'

'Yes, especially as he did it falling from the mainmast of his pirate ship.'

She had to smile at the thought. 'How wonderful it must be to have a child's imagination,' she said. She thought of Nicola's naïve questions about the letter from the hospital, and she could only guess at what was going through the girl's mind. It was all beyond her experience. Most of it was beyond Plum's too, for that matter. 'Would you like a drink, Paul?' Suddenly she wanted to talk.

'I think I could force one down.'

'Come and join me.'

They were both happy with wine so Plum picked up a bottle of Merlot and they took it into the sitting room.

'It may be wrong of me,' said Plum, 'but it seems to me that whilst you can't help loving your children there are times when they drive you mad.'

'I think you're speaking for most of us when you say that. It's been my experience, anyway.'

'That's a relief.' She told him about Nigel's phone call. 'My first thought was that he was becoming increasingly like his father, but that's unfair. Nigel can be insensitive but at least he's honest. He has that in his favour.'

'Presumably your husband was less than honest?'

'Quite a lot less,' she confirmed. 'He did for deviousness what Shylock did for credit control.' She added suddenly, 'This is my first husband we're talking about.'

'Of course.'

'Tom was everything he wasn't. He was straightforward, reliable, and above all, faithful.'

Paul settled back comfortably in his chair. 'When did you meet Tom?'

'Nearly forty years ago. He was working for my agent at the time, and we knew lots about each other by the time we got together. It was very easy.'

Paul nodded. It was one of the things Plum liked about him. He either nodded or prompted but he never tried to take over the conversation.

'I just couldn't believe it at first, you know, in hospital after the accident. They took me to him. I was still bandaged up after the operation but that didn't matter. I just remember the screen-thing that monitors the heart and everything else. They were taking it away because he didn't need it any longer. I couldn't accept it though. I insisted on talking to him. It was some time before it came home to me that he was never going to speak to me again.' She refilled their glasses to cover her distress, and was relieved when Paul spoke.

'When did you realise your hand and arm would never recover?'

'Not until the second operation. The surgeon was very frank with me.' She remembered that period very well. 'You know, when I'm on a motorway and I see those foreign juggernauts I get very angry and I have to remind myself that they're not to blame. The driver who caused the accident no doubt paid a heavy penalty, and he'll have to live with the memory for the rest of his life.'

Paul was nodding again and it was strangely comforting.

'I'm sorry,' she said. 'I invited you in for a chat, not so that you could hear my sob story.'

'Don't worry about it. I've been thinking about your arm lately. Does the name Paul Wittgenstein ring any bells?'

'Oh yes, a whole peal of them. He returned from the Great War minus his right arm and had to make a career with his left....' She stopped awkwardly. 'I expect you know all that, or you wouldn't have mentioned him.'

'Yes, but I was wondering if anyone had written anything for the right hand.'

'Oh, there's lots of repertoire for either hand and specifically for the right as well. I went through all that. The problem is that it's basically twentieth century music.'

'Some pianists specialise in contemporary music, though, don't they?'

'They do, but that's not me, I'm afraid. A big part of me was the *virtuosa*. My world was that of Chopin, Liszt, Brahms, Rachmaninov—'

'Your Rachmaninov One is superb. It was the first one I bought.'

'Bless you, Paul. You're very kind.' She picked up a CD from the coffee table. 'Nicola and I were listening to this earlier this evening. It's Uncle Hugh playing some of Chopin's *Preludes*. Would you like to hear one of them?'

'Oh, yes.'

'Have you a preference?'

'Is the last one on there, the C sharp minor?'

'It certainly is.' She inserted it into the player and they sat back to listen, completely absorbed in the haunting arpeggio passages, sometimes gentle but developing into waves of surging passion before giving way to a delicate cadenza.

'What a beautiful touch he had,' said Paul. 'When did he record it?'

'Nineteen-twenty-nine. It's been superbly re-mastered but it's still unmistakably of the period.'

'There was a different style of playing then, wasn't there?'

'Yes, they took more liberties than performers do nowadays. For one thing, the *tempo rubato*, the massaging of the tempo between the bar lines, was more marked. I think sometimes that it was no bad thing. Performances are very streamlined nowadays, and I think they lose something because of it.' She filled their glasses again, pleased that the conversation had taken a positive turn.

'There's one thing I don't understand,' said Paul. 'How did he come to do this? I was under the impression he taught in a grammar school.'

'Oh, he went on to have quite a career as a performer. They both did, and it began apparently at Aunt Ellen's suggestion.'

8

After a few days the pain in Hugh's knee was no more than an unpleasant memory but the insomnia that had become part of his life caused him to cat-nap through the day. It was a sleep pattern that was neither restful nor good for his state of mind, as he was soon aware.

'Wake up, Major Linthwaite.' A hand was squeezing his wrist, and he couldn't place it because it was a live hand belonging to a live person with a voice, and a woman's voice at that. 'Wake up,' the voice was saying. 'It's all right. You're only dreaming.'

Hugh opened his eyes to the bright light and blinked rapidly. After a few seconds he became reoriented and recognised the owner of the voice. She was a welcome sight.

'Nurse Hepworth,' he said at last, 'I must have dozed off.' Perspiration running into his eyes made him blink again, so that for a few seconds the welcome sight was blurred. He was just relieved to be awake, although he felt drained and shaken.

'You were having a bad dream.' She poured water into a tumbler for him. 'It's nothing to be ashamed of.'

When he had relieved his dry mouth he was able to speak more easily. 'A bit of nonsense, Nurse Hepworth. That's all it was.'

'You're soaked through,' she told him, as though it were his fault. 'Open wide.' She placed a thermometer under his tongue and took his wrist to check his pulse. The warm physical contact was reassuring. On an impulse he touched the back of her hand and found it smooth and soft despite the rigours of her work.

'Major Linthwaite, you mustn't do that.'

With the impediment of the thermometer beneath his tongue he made what he hoped was an apologetic sound and withdrew his hand. She noted his pulse and temperature and said, 'I'll be back in a minute. We'll have to bathe and change you.' She returned his notes to the foot of the bed before leaving the room. The perspiration had cooled and his pyjamas and sheets stuck to him like a wet cocoon.

After some minutes the door opened again and Nurse Hepworth backed in with a trolley, followed by another nurse carrying clean linen. Together they administered the bed bath, finally making up the bed with new sheets.

'There.' Nurse Hepworth turned down the collar of his clean pyjama jacket, even though he could have done it quite easily for himself. 'Now you're clean and smart again, ready for your visitor.'

'Thank you, both of you.' He was puzzled. 'Did you say I had a visitor?'

'Yes, a lady telephoned to ask about visiting hours. She said you were expecting her.'

As soon as they were out of the room he took a letter from his bedside table to read it again. It was dated the 18th November.

Dear Hugh,

Thank you for your reply. Of course I was serious when I offered to visit you. I'm coming into Leeds on Tuesday to see my dressmaker, and it seems an excellent opportunity to come and see how you're recovering after the operation. If there's anything you need, do write and tell me and I'll bring it along.

Yours truly and with all good wishes,
Ellen Bainbridge.

He'd remembered her offer of a visit, but he hadn't taken it at all seriously. Setbacks had been so much a part of his life for the past six years, he'd wondered how serious she was about coming to see him, but now it seemed that the visit was about to take place.

At two-thirty Nurse Hepworth came in to check that he was presentable. 'Major Linthwaite,' she announced, 'you have a visitor.' She stood aside to allow Ellen into the room and then left.

'Ellen,' he said, taking her hand, 'How marvellous of you to come. Please take a seat.' He motioned towards a chair by the side of his bed.

'You sound surprised,' she said. 'You knew I was coming.'

'Not surprised,' he lied, 'just delighted.'

'Good. Well, how are you? I imagine it all went well?' She took off her coat and draped it over the back of her chair. He noticed that her dress was dark blue with yellow braid around the collar and it went remarkably well with her brown curls and light complexion.

'They tell me it was a success,' he said. 'They took a quantity of shrapnel from my knee and I'm much more comfortable, although I haven't tried standing yet. That's the next stage.'

'Oh well, I'm glad things have gone well so far.' She lifted a bag on to her knee and searched through it, 'I didn't know what to bring you. You're very undemanding, you know. I couldn't remember if you smoked, so I didn't bring you cigarettes or tobacco.'

'I don't smoke very much, and they're rather strict here about when and where.'

'Are they really?'

'It's a military hospital,' he reminded her, 'run by Queen Alexandra's Imperial Military Nursing Service, and let me tell you, they're more demanding than drill sergeants.'

'How awful. Don't they mop your fevered brow and hold your hand as they do in the pictures?'

'The spangled brow gets the odd swipe with a sponge, I have to admit, but the holding of hands is strictly forbidden. They address us by our wartime rank and then treat us as overgrown children.'

'That's a shame and absolutely no way to treat a musician and a gentleman.' She rummaged in her bag again and produced a package tied with ribbon. 'Do you like crystallised fruits?'

'Oh yes, thank you. This is ever so good of you. Let's open them and we can both indulge ourselves.' He untied the ribbon and wrapping paper.

'I thought you might like something to read as well, and I didn't know what, so I brought you some past issues of *Monthly Musical*

Record.' She smiled self-consciously. 'I don't know why. It's rather dry, isn't it?'

'I'll have you know,' he told her with theatrical dignity, 'it's my favourite bedtime reading.' He offered the opened box of crystallised fruits to her and she took one.

'Well, I did wonder, and I thought you might like to borrow this as well.' She handed him a small, dark-red volume, which he opened at the title page.

'*Voices of the Night,*' he read. 'It's very kind of you to lend me this. You know, I can't think of a better way of passing the time between meals, baths and stern reprimands than by reading Longfellow.'

'Do they really tell you off?'

'I tell you, they're merciless. The nurse who showed you in is a tyrant. She doesn't let me get away with a thing, and she's a mere child. I leave you to imagine what the older ones are like. They've had longer to practise their tormenting skills.'

'She told me you needed cheering up,' Ellen confided.

'Oh? What else did she tell you?'

'Only that you've not been sleeping very well, and I must say I'm not surprised with all this going on.' She gestured vaguely in the direction of his knee.

'It's not all that bad really. As I told you before, there are many worse off.'

She nodded minutely. 'I've known a few. My brother was killed on the Somme.'

'I'm sorry.' He wanted to touch her hand but resisted the impulse. Instead he asked, 'What was his regiment?'

'The Fourteenth. He was in your battalion. I know that because I overheard you talking with the policeman in Harrison's.'

'Of course,' he said, searching his memory, 'your brother must have been Edward Bainbridge.'

'Yes.' She looked at him in surprise. 'Did you know him?'

'Only slightly, I'm afraid.'

'His company commander wrote to my parents. He said some very flattering things about him. He also said that he couldn't have suffered at all. Do you believe that's true?'

'Absolutely.' He could tell her that with confidence. 'His dug-out received a direct hit from an artillery shell. They could have known absolutely nothing, believe me.'

'But how can you be certain of that?'

'I've seen enough of them,' he told her gently.

'Thank you for telling me that.' She nodded again in the pensive way she had and then suddenly brightened. 'This is awful. I'm supposed to be cheering you up. Instead I'm depressing you.'

'No, you're not.' He thought quickly of something to say. 'You know, I never realised you were one of the Bainbridges.' It sounded ridiculous even as he said it.

'Didn't you? Don't you think my name rather gives it away?'

'I know. I meant that I didn't realise you were half of Adams and Bainbridge, the wool merchants. It was speaking of your brother that made me think of it.' And now he thought a little more about it, it explained things about her that had puzzled him.

'I'm one of them, it's true,' she said, 'but our side of the family has nothing to do with the running of the firm now that my father and brother are no longer with us.' She seemed bored with the subject because she said suddenly, 'I remember now what I wanted to ask you. I've been thinking about you and your marvellous new piano. I imagine the day can't come soon enough when you're able to go home and play it.'

'You're absolutely right.'

'I thought so, and thinking about it gave me an idea. Tell me, do you do much ensemble playing?'

'I haven't since before the war,' he said, wondering what she had in mind.

'I've heard you with Rose in school concerts.'

'Oh, I've played for pupils,' he agreed, 'but that doesn't really count, does it?'

'I think it does, because I was very impressed with your playing. As a matter of fact, I've been wondering if you might consider working with me on a recital programme.' Her eyes widened in a way that was becoming engagingly familiar. 'I think it would be rather exciting. Don't you?'

He hesitated, surprised at the step he was about to take. Finding excuses not to do things had become rather a habit. He was aware of the reason, even though the process had become almost unconscious. Ellen's proposition, however, was of a different kind. Whether the appeal was in the sheer pleasure of making music, or in the knowledge that the responsibility involved bore no relation to the kind he had come to shun, he had no clear idea. He only knew he was about to break his habit, and that he felt pleased about it.

'Yes,' he agreed, 'I think it would be an excellent thing to do.'

9

'Abbey and Tamsin are coming today.'

'Yes, I know.' The expected arrival of Paul's grandchildren was Nicola's latest excitement. Plum hoped they would get on well; Nicola needed the company of other children, whatever her parents thought. She had a selfish reason, as well, for wanting some time to herself. Her arm was particularly painful and she saw no reason why Nicola should suffer because of it. She naturally tried hard to keep her pain and frustration to herself but there was always a danger that it might get the better of her. 'Let's go through the second half once more,' she said, 'and then we'll leave it for the day. Start at "seven nines".'

Nicola took a breath, like a swimmer about to dive into a pool, and sang, 'Seven nines are sixty-three, eight nines are seventy-two, nine nines are eighty-one, ten nines are ninety, eleven nines are ninety-nine….' She stopped, inhaled again and sang triumphantly, 'Twelve nines are a hundred-and-eight!'

'Good girl! Now you know the first nine tables. Aren't you pleased?'

'Yes, but I still can't do the adding on.'

'What do you mean?'

'At school we have to do it by adding on.'

'Ah.' Realisation emerged. 'Do you mean that when you do the nine-times you have to keep adding nine to the last line?'

'Yes, I can't do it.'

'But there's no need. Just say the next line – eight nines are seventy-two, or whichever line it is, and it'll tell you the answer.'

'We have to do "three down, one to carry" and that sort of thing.' It was evidently causing her some anxiety as well as confusion.

'Oh well, let's not try to do too much all at once.' It seemed to Plum that Nicola's teacher was making the task unnecessarily difficult, but she was the expert after all, so it might be impertinent to criticise her.

'Can we do reading?'

'Do you really want to?'

'Yes, I want to know what happens to Uncle Hugh and Auntie Ellen.'

'I do too, Nicola.' It wasn't at all what Plum had expected but the child wanted to read, and that was what really mattered. She picked up an envelope from the desk and took out the letter. 'Look at this beautiful writing,' she said. 'Handwriting is usually harder to read than print but this is very clear. It shouldn't be too difficult.'

Nicola studied the letter and read ' "Dear Hugh, Thank you so much for your rec …" '

'It's a soft "c".'

' "Thank you so much for your recent letter." What's "recent"?'

'It means "not long ago". The letter was possibly a day old.'

' "I am flatt…" '

'Just read it as it looks.'

' "I am flattered that you should invite me to join you on the twenty-first, and I shall be del…." '

' "I-g-h-t" sounds like "might" or "tight".'

' "I shall be delighted to join you. Handel's…." '

'Well done.' Plum took the letter from her. 'There are some really difficult words in this letter and you've done well to read them, but I think the rest of that sentence would be too much. Basically, she's thanking him for inviting her to a performance of Handel's *Messiah*.'

'What's that?'

'It's an oratorio.' She knew that was a dead end. 'Do you know what an opera is?'

'Yes, where they all dress up and sing.'

'That's right, and an oratorio is rather like an opera but without costumes, scenery or acting. The singers just stand up and sing. *Messiah* tells the story of Jesus; the music is absolutely glorious, and if you're interested I'll let you hear some of it.'

'Why don't they dress up?'

It was a fair question. 'Long ago,' she explained, 'there was a law against the performance of plays and operas during Lent. That's the forty days—'

'I know what Lent is. We do it at school every year. The vicar comes into assembly and talks about it. Why didn't they allow it?'

'The Christian church was against it because Lent is a serious time of preparation for Good Friday and Easter. Also the church wasn't too keen on the theatre and its actors and singers in those days.'

'Why?'

Plum suspected she might have pressed one button too many. 'There was a lot of bad behaviour in the theatre,' she explained carefully, 'drunkenness, gambling and that sort of thing.'

'And women like Nell Gwynne.'

That was a surprise. 'That kind of woman, yes.'

'The King was one of her boyfriends.'

'And she sold oranges, which reminds me. Shall we get some satsumas when we go to the supermarket? I haven't tasted one for ages.'

Nicola was still locked on to the subject of relationships. 'Do you think she fancied him?'

'Who, Nell Gwynne?'

'No, silly. Do you think Auntie Ellen fancied Uncle Hugh?'

'At that stage? I don't know. They were getting on very well, so I suppose she may have.'

'She didn't say so in that letter.'

'Oh well, she wouldn't.'

'Why not?'

'A woman would never give the game away in those days. It wasn't ladylike. Relationships took much longer to develop than they do now, and there was another reason why Aunt Ellen would have to be careful not to let him think she was interested in him. I read about it recently.'

'What do you mean?'

'She was one of "Two Million Surplus Women". That's what one of the newspapers called them. It was all because of the shortage of men after the First World War. It was reckoned that about two million women would never marry, because so many young men had either been killed or were so badly injured, physically or mentally, that they could never lead a normal life. So you can see that Aunt Ellen wouldn't want Uncle Hugh to think she was trying to find a husband, in case it scared him away. It can happen when a woman appears too keen.'

'Two million sounds like a lot.' It was also beyond Nicola's imagination.

'There are sixty million people living in Britain now,' explained Plum. 'If we estimate the female population at a half of that, two million works out at one in every fifteen.' Whilst she didn't have Nicola's numeracy problem, she'd never been terribly good with figures and had already identified a flaw in her calculations. 'Actually,' she said, 'it was worse than that, because not all of the fifteen would be of marrying age. Some would be young girls or old women.'

Nicola was nodding, a gesture that Plum had learned would most likely lead to an abrupt change of subject.

'I like satsumas as well,' she said. 'Let's get some.'

Plum was happy to put the item on her shopping list. Hugh's relationship with Ellen, Handel's *Messiah* and complex mathematics could wait. Shopping for satsumas was much easier, even when her arm was driving her mad with pain.

10

Twenty-four hours after the performance they sat in Hugh's sitting room, still discussing Huddersfield Choral Society's *Messiah*.

'What could be better,' said Ellen, accepting a cup of tea, 'than the December pilgrimage to Huddersfield Town Hall?' After a moment, she added, 'Speaking of which, where are we going to have our recital?'

'Not in Huddersfield Town Hall, certainly. We'd struggle to fill Cullington Town Hall and it's a fraction of the size. I've been giving it some thought though.'

'Have you had any ideas?'

'Well, I considered the school, largely because of the piano. It would be ideal but for one serious obstacle.'

'Do you mean Mr Pickford?'

Hugh nodded. 'He's capable of giving the governors a dozen reasons why we shouldn't have the hall, and without bothering to mention his true objection.'

'He certainly seems to view you in a bad light, and I can't imagine why. More tea?'

'Yes, please.'

'I must say, Hugh, I don't know how you can drink it so hot.' She lifted the teapot and refilled his cup.

'I'm afraid it's a habit after years in the trenches, but I really should make an effort to control it.' Returning to the subject of Pickford, he said, 'To be fair to the wretched man, I'm not his only whipping boy. He extends the treatment to anyone who saw active service, basically because he spent the entire war in England with a territorial reserve battalion.'

'But my brother was a territorial and he went to the front.'

'When did he enlist?'

She spent a moment in recollection and said, 'It was about the time of the outbreak of hostilities. Why do you ask?'

'He would have to sign the Imperial Service Obligation. It meant that he could be posted abroad or to any other battalion. I enlisted as a territorial in nineteen-ten, a few months after Pickford and long before the ISO came into force, and I volunteered for overseas service. Pickford never did.'

'I see.'

'And now, doubtless feeling himself accursed and holding his manhood cheap, he assuages his inadequacy by picking on the not-so-happy few. You should see the way he treats Bertie Cartwright, and the poor chap's already vulnerable.'

'I gather Mr Cartwright also saw active service.'

'Yes, plenty. The children refer to him as "Nelson" because he lost his right eye and arm, but they respect him, whereas they call Pickford "Mary" for obvious reasons, and have no respect for him whatsoever. They're afraid of him but that's as far as it goes.'

'I can't imagine the staff respect him very much either.'

'He has his toadies among the older end, but most of us are of the same mind.' He put his cup to his lips and then, remembering his good intention, returned it to its saucer. Also, in the perverse nature of reflexes, his twitch had returned, and he put his hand to his face to hide it, even though Ellen must have noticed it.

She reached across and rested her hand familiarly on the arm of his chair. 'That hateful man is making you miserable, Hugh. I really think you should find a post in a different school.'

'That's not so easily done. People who have jobs are clinging to them, and who can blame them for that?'

'Even so, it's worth keeping an eye on the newspapers, isn't it?'

'I suppose so.' It called for the kind of enterprise Hugh had been so careful to avoid, but he had to admit that his way of life had changed recently for the better, and that alone made him more positive than before.

'Anyway,' said Ellen, 'that's quite enough about Mr Pickford. We're still nowhere nearer finding a hall for our recital.'

'There's the Wool Exchange ballroom, where the new orchestra meets, but I'm not sure how good their piano is.'

'Yes, I don't suppose it's used very often except when the Exchange Club has a function.' After a moment, she asked, 'What do you know about the piano in the Public Library?'

'I'm afraid it's not too good. I heard someone play it not long ago and I wasn't terribly impressed.' The thought seemed to lead to another, because he said with sudden enthusiasm. 'Central Hall. I've just remembered.' He was also aware that his twitch had now receded.

'What have you remembered?'

'I went to a recital there shortly after the war, and they had a very nice Bechstein.'

'You do get around, Hugh. I don't get to half as many recitals as you, but never mind. I know the building you mean, but what kind of place is it?'

'It's part of Central Methodist Church. I'm sure they'd let us use it if we gave them a donation and made a gift to some deserving cause.'

'There's certainly no shortage of charities. We could do the whole thing for a good cause if it would get us started. '

'I'm game for that.'

Ellen smiled. 'I'm just wondering what my mother would say. My family has always been high Church of England. The whole business of rivalry and schisms leaves me unimpressed, I have to say, but she's quite militant. She's also very scathing about non-conformists.'

'Would it create a problem?'

'Not in the least. She's used to me making my own decisions. According to her, I was always the *enfant terrible* of the family.'

'Surely not.'

'You don't know my mother.' The notion seemed to nudge her memory, because she asked suddenly, 'Have you any plans for Christmas?'

'Not really. The only close family I have in this country are my brother and his wife, and they have their hands full this Christmas because they're expecting an addition to the family.'

'Their first?'

'Yes.'

'How lovely for them, but as you're at a loose end, would you care to join us for lunch on Christmas Day?'

'Thank you. I'd like to very much, but how would your mother feel about it?'

'It was her suggestion. She's still getting used to there being only two of us, as I suppose I am. Also, I think she wants to look you over to decide whether or not you're a fit person to share a concert platform with her impressionable daughter.' There was fun in her eyes when she asked, 'You're not a non-conformist, are you?'

'Only in the widest sense. The army had me down as C of E, but I suppose if I had to wear a label nowadays I'd call myself agnostic.'

'I think it might be a good idea to keep that to yourself.'

* * *

On the following morning Hugh emerged from Dalton's Bookshop in the High Street carrying a copy of Longfellow's *Birds of Passage*, his Christmas present to Ellen, and he was about to seek some suitable wrapping paper for it when he heard his name being called. He recognised the voice immediately as that of Bertie Cartwright, but he turned carefully because his knee was not yet fully healed. 'Good morning, Bertie,' he said.

'Good morning, Hugh.' Bertie eyed the small parcel. 'Laden with shopping, I see.'

'Fairly staggering,' said Hugh, 'and in need of respite. Does coffee appeal?'

'Most strongly. Harrison's?'

'Where else?'

They walked the fifty yards or so to Harrison's Coffee House, and on the way Bertie remarked, 'You're walking better. You've improved in the last few days.'

'Much better,' agreed Hugh, 'although I still carry a cane, just to be safe.'

'Very wise.' They touched their hats in response to a salute from a man wearing an army cap and shabby civilian clothes. Hugh recalled him only vaguely, and thought he might have known him at Ypres.

As they entered Harrison's, Bertie said, 'We live in hopes, Hugh.'

'Of what, exactly?'

'Of finding ourselves in the utopia Lloyd George promised us, the "Land Fit for Heroes". God knows, not every man was a hero but they all deserve better than that. Frankly, it appals me to see an ex-soldier in that state, and you never have far to look for one.'

'Quite.' Hugh hoped Bertie wasn't about to have one of his introspective spells. They came upon him with little warning, and the melancholy that followed them lingered sometimes for days. Fortunately, a man in morning dress provided a temporary distraction by offering assistance.

'A table for two, please,' said Hugh, 'just for coffee.'

'Certainly, sir. Would you care to come this way?' The man led them to a table not far from the one Hugh and Ellen had occupied two months earlier, and left them with the list of beverages.

'I heard recently about a chap from my company,' said Bertie. 'He'd joined straight from school, had a bloody awful time on the Somme too, and saw his future in the ranks of the unemployed.' He appeared to dwell on that thought for a few moments.

'What happened to him?' Hugh imagined he already knew, and was searching for a way of changing the topic without appearing unsympathetic.

'He shot himself.'

'I was afraid he might.'

Bertie narrowed his eyes and then opened them as if he'd thought of something new. 'I'd never do that,' he said finally.

'I should hope not. Better not to think of it at all, really.'

'No, Hugh, you misunderstand me. I mean I'd never use my revolver.'

'No?'

'No, it's too messy. I'd hate anyone to find me in that state.'

Hugh was about to point out that in such a case appearances would cease to matter, but he naturally left the thought unspoken. Instead, he glanced at one of the potted palms and found inspiration. He smiled.

'What's the joke?' Bertie's eyes searched the room for a clue.

'It was a story I heard, about a chap who'd served with the East Lancashires in Mesopotamia. He walked into a restaurant one day after maybe one stiffener too many, took one look at the palms and walked straight out again muttering, 'Those bloody things must have followed me all the way from Baghdad.'

A waitress came and Hugh ordered a pot of the house blend. When she had gone, Bertie asked, 'Did you really hear that story or did you just make it up?'

'Does it matter as long as it raised a smile?'

'Not in the least. You're quite right, Hugh. It doesn't pay to be too serious.'

'But what of the present? Are you prepared for your journey into darkest Lancashire? Got your passport and currency?' The two had been friends from school; they had served in the same regiment, although in different battalions, they spoke the language of the trenches but rarely discussed the war, and Hugh usually knew when Bertie was at his most vulnerable. It was as well he was going to spend Christmas with his sister and her family in Pendle.

'I'm ready,' he said, 'but what about you? Are you going to stay with your brother again?'

'No, I have an invitation to lunch with Ellen and her mother, and I must say I'm looking forward to it.'

'My word.' Bertie's smile was a welcome sign. 'Things are evidently moving on between you two.'

'Not at all. It was simply a friendly gesture on their part. I think, as well, they're still coming to terms with the loss of Ellen's father and brother, and a guest at the family table must go some way towards making their absence less poignant.'

The waitress set the coffee things on the table and Hugh waited for Bertie to pour the coffee. It was important to let him do as much as possible with his remaining arm.

'Thank you, Bertie.' Hugh took his coffee and peered at the plate of biscuits. 'Harrison's Shortcake,' he observed. 'Excellent.'

'Don't look now,' warned Bertie, 'but the trench is about to be raided.'

As Pickford and his wife came into his field of vision, Hugh rose to greet them. 'Good morning, Headmaster. Good morning Mrs Pickford. I trust you're both well.'

'Well enough, thank you.' Pickford said to his wife, 'You know Linthwaite, of course, but have you met Cartwright, one of our English masters?'

'I don't think I have.' Mrs Pickford extended her gloved hand with more cordiality than her husband could muster. 'How do you do, Mr Cartwright?' Then, when the courtesies were complete, she said, 'Please excuse us. The Colonel and I have some shopping to do and last-minute cards to post. I hope you both have a very happy Christmas.' As they were leaving, Pickford said, 'I'll need to speak to you two next term. It's about a plan I have in mind but I'll tell you about it then. Good day to you both.'

'Well,' said Hugh when they had gone, 'at least Mrs Pickford wished us a happy Christmas. I suppose we'll find out in due course about that scheme of his.'

Bertie sighed in disgust. 'He wants to start up the OTC again. I overheard him talking about it with Baxter.

Hugh wasn't at all surprised; he'd expected as much. The Officer Training Corps would become another achievement for Pickford to set before a board of governors who had never heard a shot fired but who would no doubt share his enjoyment of the ensuing parades and pageantry. 'Don't worry, Bertie,' he said. 'We don't have to get involved.' He smiled as another thought came to him. 'Mrs Pickford said they had cards to post,' he reminded Bertie. 'Can you imagine Pickford sending messages of goodwill? What could have brought that about, I wonder?'

'It would be a tall order even for three spirits.'

'Strictly speaking, there were four. You mustn't forget Jacob Marley. As I recall, he was in the vanguard of that operation.'

'It would be a daunting task for a regiment of ghosts.'

'I once heard of a chap who underwent such a change,' said Hugh. 'He was a passed-over major in the Gloucesters, a disappointed and embittered man with scarcely a kind word for his fellow officers and none at all for his men. He was a hopeless case, they say, until one day in March nineteen-fifteen.'

Bertie smiled weakly, having an inkling of where the story might be leading.

'It happened at Neuve Chapelle. I'm told there was a bright light and a voice from above. Of course, that could have been a star shell and someone simply venting his feelings, but let's not be dismissive, because the story goes that the man suddenly became quite human. 'Follow me, lads,' he shouted as he leapt over the parapet. 'I know I've been a miserable bugger and I'm heartily sorry for it.'

'What happened to him then?'

'He was never seen again, although no one really cared. They were just glad to see the back of him.'

'It's just a pity,' said Bertie, 'that there's never a bright light and a voice from above when you need them.'

'A great pity.' It was clear to Hugh that the time would come when someone would have to stand up to Pickford. Meanwhile, though, his immediate concern was for Bertie.

11

'I can handle entertaining when it's like this.' Plum stretched out her legs and surveyed the used dishes on the garden table with complete satisfaction. Nicola and Paul's two granddaughters, Abbey and Tamsin, were indoors, applying make-up and dressing one another's hair. She couldn't imagine what the results would be but at least they were doing it fairly quietly so that she and Paul could finish the wine in peace.

'When it's like what?' Paul returned his camera to his bag.

'When it's like me buying the food and you coming over and cooking it.'

'I can see why that appeals to you.'

'How did you penetrate the mysteries of *haute cuisine*?' It was an ingenuous question from one who could only wonder at such things.

'I had to. When I found myself alone and hungry I reached for a recipe book. I've always relied on books, you see. There are manuals for everything, including cooking.'

'Do you watch those cookery shows on television?' Plum imagined someone must watch the wretched things, or the TV people wouldn't keep producing them in such irritating numbers.

'I watch some, but not the competitions. I can't see the fun in someone being reduced to tears because she's been "sent home" like a child who's misbehaved at a party. I don't know what that has to do with cooking or entertainment. Some of the other shows are okay.'

'Good, I'm glad it's not just me.'

'No, you're in good company.' He lifted the bottle. 'More wine?'

'Go on, you've talked me into it.' She let him refill her glass.

'Honestly though, cooking helped me through the early stages of widowhood.'

'I'm glad it did, but is that a word widowers use?'

'Yes, it's a unisex term. I checked it with a dictionary.'

'You actually consulted a dictionary to describe your marital status?' She eyed him with amiable disbelief.

'Why not? I didn't know what to call it and I didn't want to look a fool.'

'Fair enough. I wonder if there's a word for a widow who's also a washed-up pianist.'

'I'd describe you as a recovering widow and a temporarily washed-up pianist. No dictionary is equal to that.'

'Fate has had its final word, Paul,' she said, touching her useless arm, 'and the word isn't "temporary".'

'I'm not so sure.'

'You still see me making a one-armed return to the platform, don't you? I tell you it's not going to happen.' She put her glass down a little too heavily, because he said, 'All right, let's leave that topic.' He settled back in his chair and said, 'Tell me instead about your great-uncle. Are you any nearer finding out how he blotted his copybook with the family?'

'No, unless it was simply that he chose to follow a precarious career. I remember that being mentioned.' She smiled at a stray thought and said, 'Some people just can't cope with a rebel. He told me his relationship with Aunt Ellen's mother wasn't exactly easy. I think he made the mistake of having an opinion rather than allowing her to supply him with one.'

'That puts the blame squarely on her shoulders. What family did he have?'

'As far as I know he only had two brothers. One had something to do with tobacco farming in Rhodesia, so he wouldn't have much contact with him, but he had another in England, who was very conventional. I know that because he was my grandfather.'

'What about his parents?'

'Didn't I say? They both died in the flu epidemic at the end of the war. Uncle Hugh's father was a doctor, a local GP, so I imagine he'd be one of the first in the firing line.'

Paul poured the last of the wine into her glass and said, 'His choice of career seems an odd cause for disagreement.'

'Well, I imagine security was high on most people's agenda in those days, not that anything's changed in that respect. I had a fight on my hands before my parents allowed me to do what I wanted.'

'Did that make you a black sheep too?'

'Not in itself, but that's another story.' She stood up when she heard the phone ring. 'I'd better answer that,' she said. 'It could be Nigel or Heather wanting Nicola.'

It turned out to be Nigel.

'Hello, Mum,' he said. 'How are you?'

'I'm well, thank you, Nigel. How are you?'

'Fine, thanks.'

'Heather?'

'Fine.'

'Is Matthew fine too?'

'Yes, he's fine.'

'So everyone's fine.'

'Yes.'

'That's fine, then.' It was clearly an exhausted topic so Plum introduced another. 'You'll be pleased to hear, she said, 'that Nicola has mastered the twelve-times table.'

'Oh, really?'

'The thirteen and fourteen-times beckoned, but we drew the line there. No one likes a show-off.'

'Excellent. Actually it's about Nicola that I'm phoning. The thing is, you see, I have some work to do in France and we thought we'd make it a bit of a holiday for Heather and the children, just for a week or so. It's only fair to them.'

'That's right.' She knew what he was doing. She had often done the same with him. 'You had to play with your toys while I practised,' she confessed.

'I remember there was a cage all round the piano.'

It surprised her that he remembered that. 'Underneath a grand piano is no place for a toddler,' she explained. 'They're dangerous things.'

'I didn't know that. I thought it was to protect the piano.'

'Oh dear.'

'Anyway, we'll come for Nicola on Friday if that's all right.'

It was awful that he'd thought the cage was there for the piano's protection rather than his. 'This work,' she said, 'is it to do with the Battle of Sluys or something?'

'Crécy, actually.'

'I thought so.' It was his current research project and of vital importance to him, but as far as Plum was concerned one battle was much like another. 'What will Heather and the children do while you're engrossed in medieval battlefield tactics?'

'There's lots to do. The area's full of history.'

'Oh, Nigel ....' Some things were obvious to most people but not always to her son.

'What's the matter?'

'Nicola's having a lovely time here. She's upstairs now, playing with my neighbour's granddaughters. Don't you think it would be better to give her the choice between staying here and doing the grand tour of the battlefields?'

After a brief hesitation, possibly because Plum's argument was so unexpected, he said, 'All right, if you say so. Perhaps I could speak to her now.'

'All right, hold the line.' She put the phone down and called upstairs for Nicola, who appeared a moment later, bemused and scarcely recognisable.

'Dad's on the phone,' Plum told her. 'They're all going to France and he wants to know if you'd like to go with them or stay here with me. I'll leave you to talk to him.' She went outside to rejoin Paul, confident that she knew what the answer would be.

'Sorry I was so long,' she said. 'Nigel's not usually a great one for conversation. He says it's because I neglected him when he was a child. We've just been discussing it.' She made brief eye contact to satisfy herself that Paul was awake. 'The reason for the lengthy exchange on this occasion is that he wants Nicola to amuse herself by looking at French churches while he does some research.'

'It must be fairly urgent, this research.'

'I doubt it; it's just central to his existence. He's a medieval historian.'

'Is he?' Paul sounded impressed. 'Surely that gives him plenty to talk about.'

'Oh, it does.' She held her glass up to the light with vague optimism but it was still empty. 'Get him started him on the Hundred Years War and it won't be long before you're reaching for a cloth to throw over his cage. It's normal conversation that defeats him.' She let Paul fill her glass from the bottle he'd just opened. He was the soul of temptation.

'Here's Nicola,' he said. 'At least, I think it's Nicola.'

'Plum?' Nicola wore a smudged lipstick smile but her expression was tentative.

'What's on your mind, cover girl?' Plum held out her arm in welcome.

Nicola said unsurely. 'I can stay with you if it's still all right with you. It is all right with you, isn't it?'

'Oh, I don't know.' She turned to Paul for his opinion, 'What do you think, Mr Watson?'

'I think the place wouldn't be the same without her.'

'Then it's decided, Nicola. Here is where you shall stay.'

Nicola looked very relieved.

'It's perhaps as well, because you do need to be where there's a ready supply of cleansing wipes and moisturiser.' Heather hardly ever wore make-up and had little use for skin-care products. 'You, Tamsin and Abbey are going to need those things when you remove your make-up.' She put her arm around her bemused granddaughter and said, 'Maybe you're a little young to be wearing that stuff, but don't worry, we'll have a session on it and then you'll know what you're doing when the time comes.'

'Haven't I done it right?'

' "Properly," not "right", and I'm afraid you are a bit of a mess, darling; in fact when you came out here you looked like a … like Nell Gwynne on a night of brisk trading.' She released her and said, 'Go and tell the others I'm coming indoors soon to clean you all up.'

'Before you do that,' said Paul, picking up his camera, 'I'd like to get some pictures of them. I'll only be a few minutes.'

'Be my guest.' Three hideously made-up children seemed an unlikely subject for a photograph, but Plum had seen some of Paul's work and had no doubt he would create an entertaining picture of them. The expression 'each to his own' came to mind and, when she thought fairly about it, the same no doubt applied to Nigel's obsession with medieval warfare and, for that matter, her unseemly interest in Great-Uncle Hugh's love life.

12

Hugh accepted a glass of sherry and took the leather armchair Mrs Bainbridge indicated. She occupied a chair with a high, straight back, and her upright posture reinforced Hugh's impression of severity. She examined the chrysanthemums and carnations that the maid brought into the room, now carefully arranged in a blue-and-white vase, and said, 'They really are lovely, Mr Linthwaite. Thank you.'

'Not at all, Mrs Bainbridge. I'm glad you like them.'

'I think it's time for me to give Hugh his present,' said Ellen, taking a small parcel from beneath the Christmas tree.

'And I have one for you,' said Hugh.

The parcels were of identical size, and the reason was apparent when they opened them. 'Good heavens,' said Ellen, laughing. '*Birds of Passage*. What a surprise, but thank you, Hugh.'

'Thank you, Ellen. It seems we're of one mind.'

Showing her copy to Mrs Bainbridge, Ellen explained, 'Hugh and I bought each other copies of the same book.'

Mrs Bainbridge glanced at the cover and said with little enthusiasm, 'Hmm, poetry.'

'Wonderful poetry,' said Ellen, no doubt nettled on Hugh's account.

For his part, he was pleased that she was wearing the dark-blue dress with yellow braid that she'd worn when she visited him in hospital. She would always be lovely in his eyes but the dress made her especially so.

'And a strange coincidence that you should both buy the same book,' said Mrs Bainbridge.' Then, changing the subject, she asked, 'Mr Linthwaite, were you related to Doctor Linthwaite, who used to practise in Cullington?'

'He was my father,' said Hugh. 'Did you know him?'

'Yes, he was a fine doctor, a sad loss.'

'Thank you, but, Mrs Bainbridge….'

'Yes?'

'Please use my Christian name.'

'Very well. I believe you were in the same regiment as my son, Hugh.'

'That's right.' Hugh had already noticed Edward's photograph on the table beside Mrs Bainbridge's chair. 'Unfortunately he wasn't in my company, so I didn't know him at all well; in fact we met only twice, as I recall.' He added, 'I'm naturally sorry for your loss.'

'Thank you. He showed such promise and he was very keen on the business, but he couldn't wait to enlist.' She kept her eyes fixed on the photograph, as if staring might bring him back to life, and Hugh struggled to find something to say that might move the conversation on to a happier level. Mrs Bainbridge's feelings apart, he really didn't want to talk about the war.

'We were saying earlier,' said Ellen, 'how warm it is for December. I went outside this morning to hear the Salvation Army sing carols and, Christmas festivities apart, it felt as if spring had arrived.'

'Highly appropriate,' said Hugh, thankful for the change of subject. 'It's something to cheer people up. Snow has its place on Christmas cards and at the North Pole but it's cold stuff when all's said and done.'

'The Salvation Army,' said Mrs Bainbridge. 'What strange ideas you adopted during your stay in London.'

'It was a formative time for me.' Ellen ignored her mother's raised eyebrow and explained to Hugh, 'I really wanted to be a VAD nurse, to do something useful, but my father wouldn't hear of it.'

'You were far too young and it wasn't right for you,' said her mother in a tone that forbade argument.

'So I was sent to stay with my great-aunt in London so that I could attend the Guildhall School of Music and she could chaperone me. Good old Aunt Agnes was a game old soul and marvellous fun to be around.'

She added mischievously, 'She was a suffragette until rheumatism got the better of her and she couldn't get about anymore.' More soberly, she said, 'I do regret not being allowed to join the VAD. When I wasn't practising or studying I used to spend my spare time at Victoria Station handing cocoa, tea and cigarettes to wounded soldiers as they were taken off the trains, but it wasn't like doing something really useful.'

'I can't agree, Ellen.' Whatever Mrs Bainbridge's feelings were on the subject and however he felt about the war as a topic for Christmas Day, Hugh felt obliged to dispel any notion of inadequacy on Ellen's part.

'From being stretchered off the battlefield to a field dressing station and then returned to England,' he explained, 'involved several days of lengthy, agonising travel punctuated by long periods of waiting. A man would arrive in London hungry, thirsty and usually in great pain. Imagine, then, how he felt when someone greeted him with a mug of tea and a cigarette. Those two trifles alone would seem like the greatest luxuries, but they were insignificant beside the knowledge that the young woman who gave them to him actually cared about him.' It wasn't a memory on which he wanted to linger so he said finally, 'Believe me, Ellen, you must have done infinitely more good than you imagine.' He was conscious that Mrs Bainbridge had been looking impatiently at him at first but now she seemed as surprised as her daughter. It was enough for Hugh, however, who said, 'But why are we talking about the war on Christmas Day of all days?'

'Quite right,' said Ellen, 'we should be celebrating.'

And so they did, and when it was all over and Ellen eventually showed Hugh to the door she said, 'I warned you about Mother, didn't I?'

'I enjoyed every minute. Thank you again.'

'Thank you for coming, and we'll see each other on Tuesday, shan't we? We need all the practice we can get.'

'Lots of it.'

'Yes, lots.' For the first time, she leaned forward to accept a kiss on her cheek. 'Until Tuesday, Hugh. Take care.'

*　*　*

They had been practising for an hour or so that Tuesday, when Ellen said, 'I've been meaning to tell you about Daniel Rosen.'

'Rosen the booking agent?'

'Yes, I met him at a drinks party yesterday. I'd never realised he was the brother of Jacob Rosen the wool merchant. It was his party, by the way.' She stopped to consider the anomaly. 'It's funny, isn't it, that Jewish businessmen hold parties around Christmas without actually believing in any of it?'

'I suppose it's a good time to get people together. I mean they're not pretending to celebrate Christmas, are they?'

'Not at all. It just seems odd.'

Hugh imagined Ellen would tell her story in her own time, and he wasn't disappointed.

'He's coming to the recital. I told him about the programme and he's free that evening. He said he'd like very much to come.'

13

Avid as usual for any news about Great-Uncle Hugh and Great-Aunt Ellen, Nicola peered over Plum's shoulder to ask, 'What is it?'

'Three things, actually,' Plum told her. 'There's the programme from one of their very early recitals, and the other thing's a letter and a contract, a written business agreement.'

'What does it say?'

'It's anyone's guess. If you ask me, legal mumbo-jumbo was even more obscure in the twenties than it is today. It seems to be a contract between Hugh and Ellen and a firm called The Daniel Rosen Agency. They found work for musicians and they were quite big at one time but they were swallowed up in the seventies like so many others. Still, it's nice to know that our favourite people found representation so quickly. Good for them.'

'How does a firm get swallowed?' Nicola struggled with figurative language.

'A bigger agency bought it. It happens all the time.' She picked up the recital programme and said, 'Good heavens, I wonder how they persuaded Daniel Rosen or one of his people to go to a recital in Central Hall.'

'What's wrong with it?'

'Nothing at all, but they'd be used to grander places than that.' She looked again at the programme. 'Even so,' she said, 'whoever it was had a rare treat. *Romance in G* by Beethoven, *Fantasy Pieces* by Schumann – I've played the *Fantasy Pieces*, but with a clarinettist. Schumann wrote them for either instrument – and *Sonata in A* by César Frank. I wish I'd been there. No wonder they managed to charm the Rosen agency.'

Knowing nothing of the music on the programme, Nicola was busy with her own thoughts. 'I wonder what it was like inside people's houses,' she said after a while. 'I mean if they didn't have fridges and washing machines and DVD players, what did they have?'

'They kept things cool in a larder or a cellar, and they listened to the radio or made their own entertainment.' As she spoke, Plum knew the question deserved a better answer. There would certainly be information on the internet but she wondered if there might be a better option.

'Mr Watson's coming over soon for coffee,' she said, 'and he's lived here for ever. We can ask him if he knows of a place where we can find out about those things.'

* * *

The notice read: Adults £5, Senior Citizens £3, Children £2.50. Plum paid for two adults and a child.

'Why did you do that?' Paul seemed faintly amused.

'These places need our financial support. In any case, I don't advertise the fact I'm a pensioner.' She consulted the leaflet and said, 'They talk about walking through two centuries but they don't say where it all begins.'

'There's a sign in front of you,' said Paul.

'What? Oh, so there is.' She handed the leaflet to Nicola and fumbled in her bag for her glasses. 'Right, let's begin at the beginning.' She looked around her inquisitively and asked, 'What was this place before it was the Cullington Folk Museum?'

'It was a worsted spinning mill until the mid-eighties, and then it was a carpet warehouse and lots of other things. It's only been a museum since the millennium.' He stopped to examine the first display, in which two manikins dressed in shabby woollen clothes were regarding a strange machine, evidently with malign intent, because two sledgehammers lay close by.

'What does it say, Nicola?' Plum drew her attention to the label.
'Can't you see it, even with your glasses on?'
'Of course I can. I want you to read it for yourself.' Plum gave Paul a shove because he was smiling at Nicola's question.
' "The Luddites",' she read. 'Is that right?'
'Yes, go on.'
Nicola read on silently, narrowing her eyes in concentration at an occasional word. Finally she said, 'The cloth ears ....'
'The clothiers,' Plum told her, 'the cloth manufacturers.'
'They had machines put in to save money by doing the work instead of the ....' She peered again at the label and read, ' ".... croppers." '
'Good girl.'
'Yes, and the croppers broke up the machines. It says somebody was killed and some of the croppers were hanged. What does that mean?'
'It was a way of putting offenders to death,' said Paul.
'That's horrible.'
'They stopped doing it fifty years ago,' he assured her.
'Good. Why were they called croppers?'
'When a piece of cloth is woven there are lots of little hairs sticking up and they have to be trimmed off. It's called 'dressing' the cloth. In those days the croppers did it with shears like those on the wall.' Paul pointed to a pair. 'But this machine did it quicker and more cheaply.' He noticed Plum regarding him with surprise. 'I've read books about it,' he explained.
'You're just full of surprises.'
They walked on and learned something of political and social reform via the Chartists' Revolt, the Plug Riots and the Ten Hour Bill, none of which appealed to Nicola's curiosity.
'At ten, you would have been a seasoned worker,' said Plum in an effort to stimulate her interest, 'probably in a woollen mill.'
' "The Factory Act gave children two hours of lessons per day",' read Nicola. 'What can you learn in two hours?'
'Basic reading, writing and arithmetic, I suppose,' said Plum. 'It must have been very basic too.'
Nicola spotted an advantage in the system. 'If everybody was as bad at reading and stuff,' she said, 'nobody would get the mickey taken out of them for not being able to do it.'

'Oh, darling, that's not going to happen anymore.' Plum took the child's hand and squeezed it. 'When you go back to school you'll impress everyone with what you can do. Just look at the way you're reading these labels. You couldn't do it before but you can now.'

'Reading's a lot easier,' agreed Nicola, 'when you think you can do it.'

'That's right. You just lacked confidence.'

'But I still don't understand maths.'

'One job at a time, Nicola.'

'Ten hours a day,' said Paul. 'They cut the maximum hours of child labour down to ten a day and that, believe it or not, was a great step forward. Poor little waifs.'

'Let's find something more cheerful,' suggested Plum.

The Education Act of 1870 failed to impress Nicola so they walked on and came inevitably to the Great War.

'It was the one Uncle Hugh was in, wasn't it?'

'That's right.'

Nicola started reading and said, 'It says "nineteen-fourteen". I thought it happened in nineteen-forty.'

'The National Curriculum has evidently done for history what it's done for western music,' said Plum anticipating a major learning event. 'We could come back to this when we've had a cup of tea.' She thought she might be equal to it by then.

'Oh, just let me read this one.'

'All right.' Recognising involvement, Plum was happy to give way.

'It says somebody was shot,' said Nicola.

'There's always a danger of that in wartime.'

'No, this is important. The Arch ….'

'The Archduke Franz Ferdinand,' prompted Paul.

'Somebody shot him and Austria went to war ….' She scrutinised the label for further information.

'Austria declared war on Serbia, and because of the web of alliances between the great powers the war became worldwide.'

'Paul, you leave me speechless,' said Plum.

'It was my favourite subject at school.'

'Evidently.'

'Actually, it's more accurate to say that it was the only subject that interested me.'

'It's certainly fired up Nicola's interest.' The child was examining a collection of medals in a case.

'Those three,' said Paul, pointing with his finger, 'are the Nineteen-Fourteen-Fifteen Star, the British War Medal and the Victory Medal, known respectively as "Pip, Squeak and Wilfred". Your Uncle Hugh's decorations are here as well, the Distinguished Service Order, and this one here, the Military Cross. Look, there's a bar on it with a crown at each end, like his, to show that it was awarded twice.'

'I'm so glad we brought you, Paul,' said Plum.

'Have you got any medals, Mr Watson?' It was an ingenuous question.

'Yes, but not war medals. There wasn't a war when I roamed the seas. I suppose it shows how good we were at keeping the peace.'

His answer seemed to satisfy Nicola, because she went on to read about the work of the military hospitals and even found a mention of Beckett's Park Hospital, which encouraged her to read further. After all, her interest in the Great War centred on Uncle Hugh, as she called him, regarding the three 'greats' as a needless distraction.

'The nurses did it for nothing.' Nicola pointed indignantly at the label in question.

'The VAD nurses did,' Paul told her. The Voluntary Aid Detachment consisted of young ladies who had never known work of any kind, so it's very much to their credit that they volunteered. The professional nurses at the front were Queen Alexandra's Imperial Military Nursing Service, as it was called then, and Queen Alexandra's Royal Naval Nursing Service.' Paul pointed out the distinctive uniforms to her.

What Nicola thought about that remained a mystery, because just then a woman's voice said, 'Hello, Nicola.'

'Hello, Mrs Bristow.' Nicola smiled at the short, stocky woman who greeted her. 'This is my gran but I don't call her that.'

'Victoria Harvey,' Plum told her.

'I was Nicola's class teacher before the holiday,' said Mrs Bristow.

'And this is Paul Watson, neighbour and innocent bystander.'

'How d' you do?' Mrs Bristow shook hands with them both. 'I've just come in for some leaflets about the Victorian display they had here earlier.'

'We're doing the Great War and its aftermath,' Plum told her. 'Nicola's very interested in it.'

'Really?'

'I'm reading a lot better now, Mrs Bristow, and I know all the times tables.' She added modestly, 'I can't do the adding on yet.'

'That's right,' said Plum. 'Nicola says you teach them to learn the tables by addition. I must say it sounds very strange.'

'Oh, I know.' Mrs Bristow was almost apologetic. 'Ofsted insist that they understand the theory behind everything. Learning by heart isn't good enough.'

Plum considered the matter for a moment and said, 'Is that what we pay them for?'

'That sort of thing,' confirmed Mrs Bristow. She looked at the nursing display and said, 'So you're interested in the Great War, Nicola?'

'Mm, my Uncle Hugh was in it.'

'Her great-great-great-uncle, actually but Nicola feels quite close to him now she's learned more about him,' said Plum.

'Nicola has a lively imagination.' Mrs Bristow smiled. 'She told me one of her grandparents was a concert pianist.'

'If only that were still the case,' said Plum. 'Unfortunately an accident robbed me of that livelihood.'

Mrs Bristow put a hand to her mouth. 'I'm sorry,' she said. 'I'd no idea.'

'It's an easy mistake to make,' said Plum. 'Mind you, it's not true about her granddad being an astronaut.'

'No?'

'He hated flying.'

'Of course....' She smiled self-consciously when she recognised a leg-pull. 'Anyway, I'm delighted to hear about Nicola's progress and I've enjoyed meeting you both.'

Nicola was looking worried. When Mrs Bristow was gone she said, 'I never told her Granddad was an astronaut.'

'I know you didn't and she knows you didn't.'

'It was just Plum being silly,' said Paul. 'You'll get used to it.'

They reached the end of the Great War and entered the domestic scene.

'Look,' said Plum, 'there's a peggy tub and a posser. There's a rubbing board as well.'

'A what?'

'A rubbing board. The housewife smeared soap on the clothes and rubbed them up and down that board and then put them into a peggy tub like that one, and splashed them round with a posser.' She pointed to a wooden pole that terminated in a disc with four short legs. 'Then, when she'd rinsed the clothes she put them through a mangle to wring the water out.'

Nicola's eyes grew wide as she viewed the hideous contraption. Then she transferred her attention to the corrugated peggy tub and a practical question occurred to her. 'How did she put the water into the tub?'

'That's a good question.'

Paul came to the rescue. 'She used a piggin,' he said. 'I can't see one, but it was usually a half-gallon or two-pint can with a handle, and the water was heated either in a wash-boiler that had its own fire, or in a range like that one.' He took her to look at the black iron range and explained, 'It heated the room, it provided hot water and it had a hob at the front of the fire and an oven as well.' Pointing to a device hanging from the ceiling, he said, 'That arrangement of wooden poles is a creel. She would hang the wet clothes over it to dry in the warm air from the fire.'

'Wash day must have been non-stop donkey work in those days,' said Plum, 'and after all that she would have to iron the clothes with an iron heated up on the hob, and then prepare a meal for the family.'

'I bet she was ready for bed after that.'

'Yes, and the savage amusement didn't always end there, but I don't think we'll go into that.'

'Is that how Auntie Ellen did her washing?'

'No, before she married Uncle Hugh I imagine she would have a servant to do that for her, and if Uncle Hugh didn't have a housekeeper he would send his washing to a laundry and pay to have it done. I really don't know what they did after they were married.'

'It was really hard work for whoever did it,' said Nicola.

'It was,' agreed Plum. 'I'm quite worn out at the thought of it.' She added, 'I'm also ready for a cup of tea. Are you two coming?'

14

February 1921

After a promising meeting with Daniel Rosen and a highly successful recital Hugh's sunny mood suffered a hiatus when Bertie failed to turn up at school on the following Monday, and he was even more concerned when he learned that there'd been no message from him.

'Colonel Pickford is most displeased,' Baxter told him in his fussy way.

'I've no doubt he is,' said Hugh, 'but someone needs to find out what's happened to Cartwright. Look here, I'm free after assembly. Let me go to his flat and see if he needs help.'

The Senior Master hesitated. 'Well, I suppose it should be all right. I'll just have to find someone else to take his first lesson.'

Hugh had little interest in Baxter's problems and immediately after assembly he caught the tram to the end of the road where Bertie lived. When he arrived, the housekeeper Mrs Ingham, whom Hugh had met on a previous occasion, answered the door. The landlady was at the shops, she explained, adding that she knew nothing about Bertie's indisposition.

'I suppose he'll be in bed if he's poorly,' she suggested.

'All right, let's find out.' Hugh walked down the passage and knocked on the door.

'Bertie, are you there?' There was no reply so he knocked and called again. 'Bertie, it's Hugh. Are you all right? Bertie?' He tried the doorknob but the door was locked. Turning to Mrs Ingham, he asked, 'Have you got your key?'

'Well, yes,' she said, taking a bunch of keys from the pocket of her apron, 'but I don't know if we should intrude.'

'It's important,' Hugh told her. 'Mr Cartwright is not in the best of health.' It was unnecessary to go into greater detail.

'All right,' she said, turning the key in the lock, 'but I'll let you go in first, sir. I don't want to walk in on a gentleman when he's in his night clothes.'

It had always been Hugh's intention to enter the room first and he did so with some apprehension. He called again, 'Bertie?' There was still no reply so he tapped on the bedroom door. Again there was no response.

'He'll be in bed,' Mrs Ingham reminded him.

Hugh opened the door and looked in. 'No, he's not. His bed's still made.'

Following Hugh warily into the bedroom, the housekeeper remarked, 'It's just like I left it yesterday morning, sir.' She patted the neatly turned bedclothes. 'This is how I turn the covers down. He hasn't been to bed since then.' As if realising for the first time that things were not as they should be, she asked, 'Where do you think he might be, sir?'

'If I knew that I wouldn't ….' He stopped. It was unfair to snap at the woman. She knew nothing of Bertie's problem and was trying her hardest to be helpful. 'It's a mystery,' he said finally. 'I wish I knew.'

'He might have left a note saying where he was going.'

'It's most unlikely.' It seemed a ridiculous suggestion but Hugh nevertheless returned to the sitting room to check Bertie's writing desk. It was remarkably tidy, which was no surprise as Bertie was a man of particularly tidy habits. Hugh found a well-used blotter, a pen and an inkstand but no note. In looking around the room, however, he noticed an empty whisky bottle and a tumbler beside Bertie's armchair. Knowing Bertie's drinking habits as he did, he viewed them with some apprehension. After a moment's thought he handed them to Mrs Ingham. 'Maybe you'd like to take care of these,' he suggested. Something else had taken his attention and he took advantage of her temporary absence to deal with it. The waste-paper basket beneath the desk contained several crumpled balls of paper, which he pushed hurriedly into his coat pocket to examine later. A glance at the clock on the mantelpiece told him that he had twenty minutes before his lesson, but first he had to check Bertie's coat rack, which was behind the door. There he found his friend's everyday mackintosh, his oilskin coat and his British Warm, but the thorn-proof tweed overcoat that he wore when walking on the moors was missing from its hook. The discovery led him back to the bedroom and the wardrobe, where he found a pair of black Oxford brogues polished as usual to a commendable sheen, itself a challenge for a one-armed man, and the curious patent clamp-arrangement that facilitated the tying of shoelaces. Bertie's brown Oxfords and, more significantly, his walking boots were missing.

* * *

At twelve o'clock Hugh responded to a terse note from Pickering demanding his immediate presence. He was not surprised to find the Headmaster in an irascible mood.

'Why did you absent yourself from work this morning, Linthwaite?'

'I went with Baxter's permission to Albert Cartwright's residence to find out if he needed help.'

'And?'

'He wasn't there. I have to confess, I'm concerned about him. He's not in the best of health—'

'You're concerned about him.' Pickford made it sound like the most ridiculous thing he had ever heard. 'He's let the school down, he's let the Board of Governors down, he's let me down, he's let his colleagues and pupils down, and you say you're concerned about him. You astound me, Linthwaite.'

Hugh realised by this time that Pickford's vile temper was the result of more than Bertie's mere absence. He thought of the unfinished attempts at a resignation letter he'd found among the waste paper that morning and wondered if Bertie had actually sent in his notice. He had to ask, 'In what way has he let you down, Headmaster?'

Pickford confirmed Hugh's suspicion by picking up a letter and brandishing it almost in his face. 'While you were playing nursemaid to Cartwright,' he said, scarcely able to contain his anger, 'the Chairman of the Governors brought this to me. Your friend has terminated his employment here and has not had the decency to serve his notice. That's what he's done.'

'May I see that, Headmaster?'

'See it? I suppose so.' He handed it to Hugh, his moustache quivering as he did so.

The letter was addressed to the Chairman of the School Governors, and it read simply:

Dear Sir Graham,
I wish to give one term's notice of termination of my employment at Cullington Grammar School.
Your obedient servant,
Albert Cartwright.

Hugh returned the letter, saying, 'He gave the appropriate notice, Headmaster.'

'But in case it has escaped your attention, Linthwaite, he's not here, and that is the point I'm making.'

'We don't yet know the reason for his absence, Headmaster.' Hugh was making a considerable effort to control his anger whilst Pickford felt himself under no such constraint.

'Damn it, Linthwaite, must you call me that? I'll remind you that I once held the rank of lieutenant-colonel and I insist on being addressed by that rank.'

'The man you're maligning volunteered for active service; he fought on the Western Front and was awarded the MC for gallantry at Aubers Ridge. He also lost an eye and an arm on the Somme.' He was aware that his twitch had returned but he continued nevertheless. 'His service record notwithstanding, Cartwright deserves better than to be condemned in his absence and on purely circumstantial evidence.'

Observing the reddening of the man's features, Hugh wondered for a moment if Pickford might fall victim to a fit of apoplexy, but eventually the man spoke, and when he did it was in controlled fury.

'How dare you, Linthwaite? How dare you speak to me in that way? Return to your duties at once! I shall decide later what I'm going to do with you.'

It was probably the most sensible option for the time being, and Hugh returned to the common room, still furious with Pickford for his attack on Bertie's character, but feeling curiously empowered by the stance he'd just taken.

Kirby, one of the Mathematics Department asked, 'What was all that about, Linthwaite? I walked past Colonel Pickford's study and there was an awful row going on.'

'Mr Pickford was playing soldiers. He's very good at it, having spent the entire war doing little else.' Kirby was one of the older members of staff, too old to serve in the war but not yet of retiring age. He was an acknowledged gossip but Hugh no longer cared what might be reported to Pickford.

'Was it about Cartwright? Colonel Pickford gave him the most awful carpeting on Friday.'

'Did he?' Hugh hadn't seen Bertie from Friday morning until the recital on Saturday evening, when he'd been too preoccupied for normal conversation.

'Well, yes, and it didn't seem to be about anything terribly important.'

Hugh wondered if Kirby spent all his free time outside Pickford's study. He asked, 'Do you know what it was about?'

'It was about a games period that Cartwright had taken for Barnes. You know Barnes is injured again, don't you?'

'Yes, but tell me about the carpeting.'

Kirby looked around him, ascertained that no one was listening and said, 'Cartwright was late bringing the boys back from the football field and Colonel Pickford tore into him about not having a watch. It really was an odd thing to get excited about, but Cartwright was in quite a state afterwards.'

Once more in his classroom, Hugh re-examined the unfinished letters, all of which began in the same way as that which had reached the Chairman, but Bertie had made two attempts at an explanation for his resignation. In two cases he had written:

I find it impossible to work under the petty

There the sentence tailed off, but in a third draft he had written more:

I feel unable to continue working under the petty and sadistic regime operated by

Again the letter was unfinished. Fair-minded as ever, Bertie must have decided to omit the reason for his decision. Still, the letter had answered one question in Hugh's mind. The remaining mystery was of Bertie's whereabouts, and Hugh had only a hunch about that.

The summons came shortly after three o'clock. Hugh knocked on the door of Pickford's study expecting a reprimand. Oddly, he no longer cared, but was nevertheless surprised to hear Pickford invite him inside in a considerably more civil tone than of late. When he entered, he found the Headmaster and also the policeman who had helped him into Harrison's Coffee House the previous October. As Pickford introduced them and they exchanged their own greetings, the resignation Hugh had felt earlier gave way to foreboding.

'I believe Mr Albert Cartwright of Alma Road was a close friend of yours, Mr Linthwaite.'

Hugh felt his stomach contract at the constable's use of the past tense. 'That's right.'

'I'm afraid I have bad news, sir. As far as we can tell at this stage, Mr Cartwright met with a fatal accident some time yesterday evening. His body was found at Ilkley Crags this morning. It's unlikely that he suffered.'

Hugh's voice was unnaturally quiet. 'What happened?'

'He was found at the foot of Hebers Gill, sir. He appeared to have fallen. Such an accident would be no surprise in the mist and low cloud we've been experiencing, sir. He could simply have reached the edge in bad visibility or slipped on a wet surface and been unable to save himself.'

Hugh had suspected the worst but he was still stunned. 'Poor old Bertie,' he said eventually. 'What an awful end.'

'I'm sorry, sir. Mr Cartwright's sister Mrs Fawcett gave us your name. She said you'd been friends for a long time. Actually, you may be able to help us.'

'In what way?'

'When did you last see Mr Cartwright, sir?'

'On Saturday evening at Central Hall in Park Street. I took part in a music recital there. Mr Cartwright was in the audience.'

The constable made a note and asked, 'How did he seem to you at the time, sir? I'm talking about his mood.'

'He seemed fine, although I confess I was quite preoccupied at the time. Why do you ask?'

'Mrs Fawcett told Ilkley Police that Mr Cartwright was taking prescribed medication for a nervous condition. Did you know that?'

Hugh nodded. 'You were in the war, Constable; in fact you were in his battalion. You know about that kind of thing.'

'I do, sir, but we have to take our evidence from independent sources.' He referred to his notebook and asked, 'Was Mr Cartwright a heavy drinker, sir?'

'Not normally.' It was strictly true; Bertie only drank to excess at moments of great anxiety but Hugh was determined not to give too much away. He asked, 'Why are you asking these questions, Constable?'

The policeman closed his notebook and returned it to his pocket. 'As I said, sir, the likelihood is that Mr Cartwright's death was the result of a tragic accident but we have to rule out, if we can, the possibility that he took his own life. Evidence will be put before the Coroner and it will be for him to determine the cause of death.'

Pickford had been silent during the interview but now he spoke. 'It would be most unfortunate for the school,' he said, 'if there were any suggestion of suicide.'

The constable gave him an admonishing look. 'Evidence is evidence, sir. It cannot be changed for the sake of convenience.'

'Of course not.' Pickford retracted guiltily. 'I simply feel that it would be unfortunate for all concerned.'

'But hardly as unfortunate as the ending of a young man's life. We must remember that, sir.'

* * *

Ellen laid her violin in its case, satisfied that no further work was possible with Hugh in his current state of mind. 'Of course, I hardly knew him,' she said, 'but he seemed quite collected when he left us on Saturday evening.'

'He would. Bertie would give no appearance at first that anything was troubling him but it would fester in his mind until he sank further and further into melancholia. He would sometimes drink as well, and that made him worse.'

'Was he always like that?'

'No.' Hugh shook his head decisively. 'It was the war.'

'And of course you men don't talk about the war.'

'It's better not to.'

She knew better than to argue. 'You mentioned his boots and outdoor clothes. What did they tell you?'

'Sometimes he would walk on the moors for solitude and to think his own thoughts. As soon as I saw they were missing I knew where he'd gone. I just couldn't understand why he hadn't turned up at school. He'd always behaved responsibly toward his colleagues and pupils. That's why I was so furious when Pickford accused him of letting everyone down.'

She smiled and said, 'Well, it looks as if your outburst has been forgotten, at least for the time being.'

'He can sack me for all I care. I could probably make a living from piano teaching, although I might need to reduce Mrs Naylor's hours. I should be very reluctant to do that,' he admitted.

'Thank goodness it hasn't come to that yet.'

'Yes, the most important thing is that the Coroner doesn't suspect suicide.'

'That really matters to you, doesn't it?'

'It's vital. Suicide, believe it or not, is still a crime. He wouldn't get a decent funeral, he certainly wouldn't be buried in consecrated ground and, frankly, he deserves better than that.'

15

'Chopin's waltzes are really parlour pieces.'
'Some would describe that as sacrilege,' protested Paul.
'You know how I feel about Chopin. I'm just saying the waltzes are at the shallow end of his output.'

They sat in Paul's kitchen, enjoying his coffee and Plum's homemade biscuits but their conversation had left Nicola stranded. She asked, 'What's a waltz?'

'It's a dance,' Plum told her. 'It has three beats in a bar – one, two, three, one, two, three.'

'Let's show her,' said Paul, standing up and offering his hand to Plum. 'May I have the pleasure?'

'You're forgetting my useless arm.'

'You don't need it. Rest it on mine.'

'All right, but let's move away from the table.' They found a space and Paul took her in hold. He began to sing the melody of the waltz song 'Tenderly.' 'Da da-da dah, da da-da dah, dah da-dah.' Nicola watched in amusement and fascination as the couple waltzed in the limited space of the kitchen and finally applauded the imaginary band.

As Paul brought Plum back to the table he said, 'You dance well. I told you the dodgy arm wouldn't be a problem.'

'I haven't danced for years. You're not bad though. Where did you learn to dance like that?'

'In a canteen at Rosyth Naval Base. I was a callow youth, awkward, shy and untutored in the ways of men and women, and the bloke who taught me was a huge, hairy stoker with tattoos all over his body. "It's easy," he said. "Every time the drummer hits the bass drum you put your left foot forward." Of course, I've refined my technique since then, but that was how it all began.'

'So that's what you did when you weren't taking photos of ships.'

'And aircraft. I was a naval airman.'

'That sounds like the product of a mixed marriage.'

'Absolutely not.' He picked up the cafetière and offered it. 'More coffee?' He refilled Plum's cup and said, 'These biscuits are very good, Plum. You could hold your head up in any branch of the Women's Institute.'

'The final accolade.' She saw the twinkle in his eye and accepted the compliment.

'Abbey, Tamsin and Henry are coming this afternoon,' said Paul, enjoying Nicola's look of delight. 'I can probably find plenty for Henry to do, so you girls can go off and do whatever you like.'

Plum asked, 'How's his broken arm?'

'It seems to be all right but he's very frustrated.'

'He has my sympathy.' Her eye fell on one of Paul's photographs, a townscape of old Cullington, the part that had so far escaped modernisation, and was reminded of something. 'Paul,' she said, 'am I right in thinking that old photos can be enhanced in some way?'

'It depends on the state they're in, but it's sometimes possible. Have you one in mind?'

'Yes, it's about ninety years old and it's rather faded but I believe it's quite sharp.'

'It wouldn't be a picture of your great-uncle, would it?'

Plum smiled self-consciously. 'My current preoccupation, yes. Actually, it's a photo of him and my great-aunt.'

'All right, let me have it and I'll see what I can do.'

'Thank you, Paul.'

Nicola was immediately excited. 'Can I see it?'

'Yes. If you'll both excuse me for a minute I'll go and get it now.'

As Plum left the kitchen, Paul asked, 'How are the lessons coming along, Nicola?'

'They're good. I know all the times tables, I can do division better now, and reading's a lot easier.'

Paul smiled his approval. 'You've worked hard and Plum's done a good job too.'

'Yes, she's really good. She should have been a teacher.'

'That would have been a sad loss for the world of music.'

Nicola considered that for a moment and said, 'She must have been really good.'

'She was brilliant.' He had an idea. 'Let me show you something before she comes back.' He selected a track from his phone and switched on the portable speaker on the kitchen counter. 'It's called "The Bumble Bee,"' he told her.

Nicola listened, spellbound at the glittering performance of the Rachmaninov transcription. As it ended, she asked, 'Was that really her?'

'I can vouch for it.' Plum's voice came from the doorway. 'Caught in the act, you two.' She added wistfully, 'I used to play that as an encore.'

'You were brilliant,' said Nicola, still overwhelmed. 'It must be really hard.'

'Oh, she could play that thing with one arm tied behind her back.'

'Paul,' warned Plum, 'you're being naughty again.'

'It was a harmless compliment.'

'Mm.' Seemingly anxious to move the conversation on, Plum handed a postcard-size photograph to Paul. Nicola stood up to look over his shoulder at the sepia portrait. She asked, 'Is that Auntie Ellen and Uncle Hugh?'

'Yes, in nineteen twenty-one, according to the note on the back. What do you think, Paul? Can you do anything with it?'

'Yes, it shouldn't be a problem.'

Nicola examined the photograph. 'She was beautiful,' she said eventually. 'I wish I could have my hair cut in a bob like that.' She added, 'and Uncle Hugh was really handsome.' She looked again and said, 'Everybody had a moustache in them days, didn't they?'

'In those days,' corrected Plum.

'Well, it made him look like somebody in one of your old films.'

'Oh dear,' said Plum, 'that's another of my secrets out in the open.'

Following On

'There's nothing wrong with old films,' said Paul. 'We must compare notes some time, but for now I think rejuvenating your ancestors takes precedence.'

* * *

Paul arrived shortly after two o'clock with the finished copy of the photograph and a peeved grandson. 'This is Henry,' he said. 'He'll have to shake hands with his left, I'm afraid. Henry, this is Mrs Harvey.'

'How do you do, Henry?' Plum took his left hand in her right. 'My word, that plaster cast looks as if it's been signed by a cast of thousands. It must be heavy as well.'

Whether through shyness or the mood of the moment, Henry made no response, so Paul said, 'The girls are doing girlie things and Henry takes a dim view of having no one to play with. He'll have to be patient for a minute, though, because I want to show you this.' He handed her the photograph, which she took with an exclamation of delight.

'Paul, you're a wonder. This could almost have been taken yesterday. It's wonderful but it must have cost you something and I don't want you to be out of pocket.'

Paul shook his head. 'It cost me a sheet of paper and you're welcome to that.'

'Well, thank you. I do appreciate it.'

'I enjoyed doing it. They're a handsome couple.' He transferred his attention to Henry, who had seemingly become mesmerised by the piano. He looked up at Paul and asked, 'What is it, Granddad?

'It's a piano. Mrs Harvey used to play the piano for a living.'

Henry looked doubtful. 'It isn't like the piano at school.'

'Ah,' said Plum, 'I imagine that's an upright piano, one that comes up to here.' She indicated an approximate height with her hand.

'No,' said Henry, 'it's littler than that.' He seemed at a loss to describe it until he added, 'Mrs Dennison plugs it into the wall and plays it.'

'Oh, an electric piano.'

'No, it's a digital piano.'

Plum looked at Paul and shrugged. 'Six years old,' she said, 'and he knows more than we do.' Speaking to Henry again, she said, 'This is a grand piano and it doesn't need electricity, not that kind anyway.' She crossed over and sat at the piano to play a scale, then, recognising interest on the boy's face, said, 'Come and sit with me and we'll see if we can make some music. What songs do you know?'

Henry perched uncertainly on the end of the stool and said, ' "The Wheels on the Bus".'

'I'm afraid I don't know that one.' Plum reflected that a great many children's songs must have been written since she was at school.

' "Five Little Monkeys".'

'Oh dear.'

' "Twinkle, Twinkle, Little Star".'

'Hooray! We're in business. Shall we play it on the high notes, here?' She played four bars in the treble. 'Or on the low notes down here?'

Henry listened to both possibilities and opted for the bass end before saying, 'Mrs Dennison does it with both hands.'

'And so would I but my left hand doesn't work anymore.'

'Why?'

'I was in a car that crashed and my arm was badly hurt. You see, I'm rather like you with your broken arm, except yours will be better soon.'

'Won't yours get better?'

'No, but don't worry about it. Let's learn "Twinkle, Twinkle".' She motioned to Paul to leave Henry with her and the lesson began. Henry learned to play "Twinkle, Twinkle" by ear, and Plum answered a great many questions, eventually showing him how musicians played from printed music. He was very interested in the symbols on the printed page and asked lots of questions about them as well. Then, finding a folded sheet of card on the end of the piano, he picked it up and asked, 'Is this music?'

'No.' Plum took it from him. 'It's something I was looking at this morning. I forgot to put it away.'

It was an order of service for the funeral of Albert William Cartwright B.A. (Dunelm), M.C. at Cullington Parish Church on 22nd February 1921.

16

The guard of honour, twelve men in all, was drawn from the Eighth and Eleventh Battalions, its sergeant-major was formerly of the Eighth, and Hugh was expecting the arrival of Arthur Gillings, an officer also of Bertie's battalion, to take charge. At Hugh's side, and in his lieutenant-colonel's uniform, stood Pickford in an ill-humour as Mrs Fawcett had not asked him to speak at the funeral. Hugh was in civilian dress but wearing his medals as a mark of respect for Bertie.

'That Gillings chap is cutting it fine,' said Pickford. 'Suppose he doesn't turn up?'

'He will,' said Hugh.

'But suppose he doesn't?'

'Then I'll take charge.' He saw Ellen frown angrily at Pickford's tone but he knew he could rely on her to control her irritation.

'I think you're assuming a great deal, Linthwaite.'

'I'm following the Chief Mourner's wishes, Headmaster.' Peering through the fog, he made out a figure in a black overcoat and homburg and as the man drew closer, recognised the blue-and-white ribbon of the Military Cross. He extended his hand to greet its owner. 'Gillings? I'm Linthwaite. It's good of you to come.' The two shook hands, Hugh introduced Ellen and Gillings greeted Company Sergeant-Major Ollerenshaw, with whom he was already acquainted.

Pickford bridled. 'Aren't you going to introduce me, Linthwaite?'

'I was about to. Arthur Gillings, formerly Captain Gillings of the Eighth Battalion, this is Mr Pickford, Headmaster of Cullington Grammar School.' He was gratified to see Pickford's face turn a deeper shade of purple. 'We're going inside, Gillings. I'll leave everything in your safe hands.'

'Thank you, sir.'

Hugh offered his arm to Ellen and they entered the church.

Mr and Mrs Pickford walked to the front of the nave, and when they were some distance away, Ellen said, 'I can't bear the way that wretched man speaks to you.'

'Pay no regard. I'm immune to all that now.'

'Even so, he's unspeakable.'

They found their places and stood as the congregation rose. Hugh heard the voice of Company Sergeant-Major Ollerenshaw.

'Guard of Honour, atten-SHUN!' A dozen boots hit the stone-flagged pathway as one, and the coffin was borne into the church. Hugh felt a knot tighten inside his stomach.

During the opening prayers and the first hymn 'The King of Love,' he became increasingly conscious of Ellen's close presence. She had taken his arm again towards the end of the hymn and now squeezed it occasionally. It was an unaccustomed but welcome reminder that he was not completely alone. It was also a timely reminder, because the next item was to be his contribution. He heard the vicar announce in his elaborate way, 'A tribute will now be read by lifelong friend and fellow-officer Major Hugh Linthwaite, DSO, MC and bar, late of the Eleventh Battalion, the Prince of Wales' Own Fourteenth Regiment of Foot, the West Yorkshire Regiment.'

Hugh walked to the lectern and glanced around the congregation. Pickford, who was seated near the front, observed him with unconcealed animosity. Mrs Pickford looked no friendlier, although that was no surprise as her husband's point of view was the only one with which she was acquainted. It was a state of affairs that Hugh intended to change. That was as long as he could control the anger and nervous tension that had tormented him since Bertie's death. He looked down at his page of notes and began.

'Albert Cartwright and I met and became friends on our first day at Gilbert de Lacey School. He was a loyal and devoted friend, one of a rare breed made rarer still by the war.' To his irritation, his twitch had returned.

'After a colourful school career during which we contributed equally to the normal triumphs and upsets of school life, "Bertie", as I knew him, went on to Durham University, whereas I pursued my education elsewhere. We maintained regular correspondence, however, and I recall a letter I received from him in nineteen-ten, informing me that he had joined the Territorials. I remember that particularly because I, too, had recently enlisted. It was a feature of our friendship that we seemed to do most things at around the same time, even when we were many miles apart.' The twitch had taken control of his left cheek, so that he was obliged to speak carefully and deliberately. Concealing his growing anxiety as best he could, he continued.

'We were commissioned at about the same time and, at the outbreak of war, both volunteered for active service.' His hands had begun to tremble, and he gripped the lectern in an effort to control them.

'Bertie saw action within three months of his arrival in France, at Aubers Ridge, a particularly ill-conceived… venture, after which he was awarded the Military Cross for gallantry.' His mouth was dry and he was finding it increasingly difficult to form his words. He was aware also that he was speaking very quietly. He made a conscious effort to speak up.

'He was in action again in the First Battle of the Somme, and that was when …. It was the battle in which he was wounded … he was … wounded and eventually medically discharged.' Clammy perspiration now covered his body, his tongue felt like a pumice stone and his voice had developed an incoherent croak.

With something akin to telepathy, the vicar's warden appeared at his side with a glass of water. Muttering his thanks, Hugh relieved the dryness in his mouth and placed the glass on the floor beside the lectern.

'Bertie was already on the staff of Cullington Grammar School when I returned from the war, and I was shocked by the change I saw in him.' He took another sip of water as the croak threatened to return.

'The damage to his body was obvious enough but, as importantly, he was by now a troubled man. His mind had become deeply affected by his experiences in the war.' He was perspiring freely now. 'I ask the veterans here today to bear with me whilst I address the remainder of the congregation and say that you can have no idea of the horrors he saw and experienced in France, and it is my fervent wish that you never shall.' His mouth was dry again and he stopped to sip more water.

'School colleagues were aware that Bertie never used a whistle when on outdoor duty; neither was he ever seen wearing a wristwatch.' Here, he met Pickford's eye. 'In this respect he was no different from other ex-infantry officers of my acquaintance. There is a connection, an association of ideas, you understand, that is impossible to break, and it is one that haunts the mind mercilessly. It is like a nightmare that stalks its victim in the waking hours.' He had never imagined that he would bring himself to speak of such things, but the knowledge of what had almost certainly driven Bertie to his death had triggered an ungovernable desire to expose the truth.

'It is difficult to describe.' Perspiration was running into his eyes. He took the handkerchief from his breast pocket and wiped his forehead. 'You see, when you look at a wristwatch, all you see is the time, and when you hear a blast on a whistle you know that a train is about to leave or maybe that a referee is about to award a penalty. But those things meant something entirely different to Bertie. When he looked at a watch face or heard a whistle being blown, in his tormented mind he was giving the order he hated most.' He took a deliberate breath. 'It was the order that repeatedly led fifty innocent men over the parapet and into a storm of machine-gun fire.'

The crucially difficult part was now mercifully behind him. He took another sip of water and a deep breath.

'Bertie had much to offer. His pupils and more enlightened colleagues knew that. He cared for the children he taught and did the best he could for them. He was also scrupulously professional in his dealings with other members of staff, but at the same time he, too, had his needs. Most of all, he needed the accommodation and understanding of others.' He looked directly at Pickford, who appeared to be examining his order of service. Mrs Pickford merely avoided his eye. Across the aisle and in welcome contrast, Mr and Mrs Fawcett minutely nodded their agreement.

'It was little to ask, and to give him less than that was to fail him in the worst possible way. It was also to treat with disdain every man who served at the Front and each of those who forfeited their lives.'

Then, with the relief that comes at the end of a monumental task, he concluded, 'For the first time in years, Bertie is at rest. No one and nothing can hurt him now.' Turning to the coffin, he added, 'I salute a staunch friend, a gallant soldier and an admirable human being.' He bowed before the coffin, picked up his notes and walked back to his place, where he sat with closed eyes whilst the vicar announced the next hymn. When they stood again, he felt Ellen's hand on his arm.

* * *

'I'll make some tea,' said Hugh, closing the door behind him.

'No, you go and sit down. I'll make the tea.' In response to his look of surprise, she said, 'I know how to do it, you know.'

'I realise that, Ellen, but I'm failing in my duty as a host.'

'Fiddlesticks.' She added, 'And I know quite a lot about them too.'

Outmanoeuvred, he took her coat and hat and hung them with his on the hall stand. All he'd wanted after the funeral was to sit for a while in solitude, but Ellen's company was soothing and he was grateful to her for coming to the funeral, so he went through to the sitting room to revive the embers of the fire he'd left that morning.

As he sat at the end of the sofa watching the flames dart tentatively between the fresh coals, he wondered quite what he had achieved with his polemic outpouring at the funeral. After some thought, he concluded that if he had caused Pickford to re-examine his behaviour, even for a moment, he could chalk up a minor success. More than that would amount to a miracle.

'A penny for your thoughts.' Ellen set a tray containing the tea things on the low table in front of the sofa and knelt beside it.

'My thoughts are not worth a farthing today.'

'Oh, I'm not so sure about that.' She stirred the tea and replaced the teapot lid.

'I see you found everything,' he said, pointing to the contents of the tray.

'Of course I did. I have hidden depths.' She poured tea, added milk and handed the cup and saucer to Hugh. 'One thing puzzles me,' she said. 'If Bertie's remains are to be interred in Pendle, why was his funeral held in Cullington?'

'His friends were here, the few he had.'

'But the church was full of people.'

'They were Leeds Rifles, Eighth Battalion men. There were some from the Eleventh Battalion there as well, and Sappers, Army Service Corps and Royal Artillery. Some came to pay their respects to Bertie because they knew him; others make a habit of attending funerals. It reminds them that, grim though their lives are, they're not dead yet.'

'Poor Hugh,' she said, taking his cup and saucer to pour some more tea, 'it's been a ghastly day for you.' She handed it back to him with a grimace. 'I still don't know how you can drink tea when it's so hot.'

'I'm sorry, it's a bad habit.'

'Why did you have to drink scalding tea in the trenches?'

'It was to avoid tasting it. The hotter it was, the less we noticed the chloride of lime they used to treat the water.'

She wrinkled her nose. 'It sounds evil, but I shouldn't talk about the war, especially after this morning.'

'It's no matter.' With the tribute done he was feeling quite flat. There was no pain in recollection, at least for the time being. 'I said more about it today than I ever have. It was necessary but I couldn't help feeling guilty, self-indulgent, if you know what I mean.'

'No, I don't think I do.'

He stared into his tea, wondering how to explain something he'd simply accepted for so long. Finally, he said, 'Do you remember my telling the congregation that Bertie had known things they could never imagine? Well, it was true. Not everything was awful, you understand. There were good things, believe it or not. The camaraderie and humour, for example, were beyond price, but things did happen that are either impossible to describe or best left untold.'

'Especially to a weak and feeble woman?'

'Why do you say that?'

'In mixed company there always seems to be a vow of silence about the war, as if it were all too terrible for the delicate ears of the fair sex.'

He nodded. 'That's a part of it, certainly.'

'I saw hideous and dreadful things at Victoria Station, Hugh. They couldn't hide them from me, or from the other women.'

'I know.' He stared again into his teacup. 'But you see, reluctant though most of us are to talk about those things, there's a kind of self-indulgence in doing so, because it feels somehow like asking for special understanding.'

She made no response but simply nodded. After a while she asked, 'Hugh, what do you really think happened to Bertie?'

He was silent for a while, and then he said, 'I suppose we'll never be sure, but his mind was in turmoil when he left for Ilkley Moor. That altercation with Pickford must have been the last straw, and whether he walked over the edge deliberately or simply lost his way in the mist, the cause and the consequence were the same.' He drained his cup again. 'I just think he was too experienced a rambler simply to have blundered over the edge.'

Ellen raised herself from her kneeling position beside the table to join him on the sofa, and he was surprised when she took his hand.

'Forgive me for being forward,' she said, 'but I imagine you're feeling quite lonely.'

He was, it was true, but he'd not realised it until that moment. 'I want to thank you,' he said, 'for being with me today.'

'Think nothing of it. The funeral was ordeal enough for you. It would have been intolerable for you to have faced it alone.'

'It was worse for Bertie's sister. It's a terrible thing to live with the knowledge that he suffered as much as he did.' He added, 'I told her the gist of what I was going to say. I'd never have said some of those things without her agreement.'

'I know you wouldn't, and I'm glad you did. Judging by Mr Pickford's face at the end of the service, I'm sure he'll think twice before treating anyone the way he treated poor Bertie.'

'I didn't see him.'

'Take it from me, Hugh, he was feeling very small.' She gave his hand a gentle squeeze.

'Bertie hated injustice. It was one of his preoccupations.'

'What do you mean?'

He looked down at her hands, now wrapped around his in willing support, and told the story.

'After Aubers Ridge a member of his platoon was court-martialled for cowardice in the face of the enemy; at least, that was what they called it. It's my belief that the only real act of cowardice is the one that's wholly premeditated. In this case, the man was hysterical through shellshock, and there's nothing premeditated about that.'

'What happened to him?'

'He was found guilty and sentenced to death. It fell to Bertie to take charge of the firing squad.'

'Oh, no.'

'It was a familiar process. They gave the prisoner a large quantity of rum and the men of the firing squad had their share too. It wasn't a popular duty so the rum was very necessary; in fact Bertie, the chaplain and the doctor were probably the only sober men at the scene. At all events, after the volley was fired the prisoner was still alive. Inebriation or reluctance to be responsible for his death had spoiled each man's aim, and it was Bertie's duty to finish the job with his revolver. It preyed on his mind for the rest of his life.'

Ellen had been gripping Hugh's hand rather hard and she now relaxed her hold. 'Horrible,' she whispered.

'Yes, but it was even worse for Bertie than it was for most of us. I suppose some men are more sensitive than others, and Bertie was a gentle soul.'

She laid her head against his shoulder. 'What a beastly business it all was.'

'Most of it certainly was.' With the story told, his tone had lost its sombreness. It was time to dismiss morbid thoughts. 'It had its lighter moments,' he said, 'and it was very instructive. When all else fails I should be able to get a job in agriculture. I don't know wheat from barley but I pride myself on being something of an expert on mud.'

'Mud?' She swivelled her head upward to see that he was smiling.

'Yes, mud. There's more than just one kind, you know. There's the ordinary species we trained on in Hampshire. Now, that's good quality mud but after a while there tends to be an unsatisfactory sameness about it. Then there's the dark, dense variety we encountered around Ypres. That does vary, usually in depth, as I recall. My favourite, however, is the rich, red, clinging mud of the Somme Valley. I always felt, you know, that it could have been put to better use.'

She looked up again and said, 'I like to hear you joke about things. It hasn't been possible recently.'

'Oh, we shall laugh again after a while.'

'But you do feel better, don't you?'

'Yes, thanks to you.' He extricated his right arm, which had become pinioned between them, and said, 'I should warn you, however, that in sitting with me on this sofa you are placing yourself in some peril, because I am a man with a past.'

'I know, I've been hearing about it today.'

'I'm referring to my Bluebeard past.'

'You make it sound so exciting.' She leaned forward so that he could slip his arm round her shoulders.

He kissed her softly on the cheek at first, until she turned her head slowly, bringing their lips inevitably together. After the ordeal of the morning, that intimacy, her nearness and the softness of her body beneath the worsted fabric of her dress were the perfect consolation.

After some time, she said, 'Does this mean we're now doing that cosy, conventional thing they call "walking out together"?'

'Only if you're of the same mind.'

'I think I must be. I wouldn't let just anyone kiss me like that.' She assumed a thoughtful pose. 'Now I think of it,' she said, I've never been kissed like that, whatever my mother might imagine, so I think that rather confirms it.'

17

'Baking stuff again,' observed Nicola as she dropped a bag of caster sugar into the trolley. 'I like it when you bake….' She hesitated.

'I detect a silent "but".'

'I don't want you to do it just for me.'

'I eat the stuff as well, and so does everyone else who comes to the house. It really isn't just for you, precious though you are.'

Nicola gave her a long-suffering look. 'You know what I mean. You're ten times better than any granny I can think of.'

'So you keep telling me, Nicola, and I appreciate it. I just can't help wondering if Princes William and Harry would agree with you. What you've just said could be construed as treason.'

'Don't be silly. Anyway, as long as you're doing it for the right reason, that's okay.'

'Hm.' Plum picked up half-a-dozen large eggs and lifted the flap to inspect them. 'You're ten years old, Nicola, and there are times when I could be forgiven for thinking you're forty.' She thought of Nigel and said, 'Maybe it runs in the family.'

With the last item on the list ticked off they headed for the checkout and transferred their shopping to the belt. Nicola took her place at the end, ready to place it in bags.

'That's twenty-three pounds ninety-one,' said the checkout assistant, watching with polite amusement as Plum opened her purse with her right hand and Nicola delved inside it for the money. 'That's a grand little helper you've got there,' she said, handing the change to Nicola.

'My daughter,' said Plum.

'Lovely.'

Nicola waited until they were outside before stopping the trolley and asking, 'Why did you tell her that?'

Plum shrugged. 'She believed me, and I feel much better about myself than I did five minutes ago.' She helped push the trolley to the car and said, 'You should try giving yourself little treats now and again. It'll do you a power of .... Oh hell.'

'What's the matter?'

'We have a puncture. I'll have to phone the AA.' She rested her bag on the bonnet of the car and was searching for her mobile phone when a man returning to the van next to them said, 'I see you've got a flat tyre, love.'

'Yes, I'm calling the AA.'

'Nay, put your phone away. I'll change it for you.'

'Will you really? Thank you, that's very kind of you. I'll open the back so that you can get to the jack and things.'

The man grinned. 'Leave 'em be. I've got a man-size jack in t' van. I'll get t' spare wheel out though. 'Alf a tick.' He opened the rear doors of his van and produced a wheel brace and a trolley jack, which he placed under the rear axle. As he loosened the wheel bolts he looked up and saw Nicola watching him. 'Now then, love,' he said, 'you'd better take notice and then you'll be able to do it another time.'

Nicola nodded earnestly.

'Only joking, flower. A pretty lass like you will always have a strong lad to do it for you.'

He changed the wheel and slid his jack out from under the car. 'Right, love,' he said to Plum, 'the job's a good 'un.'

'Thank you so much. You've been very kind.'

'You're welcome, love.' He returned his jack and wheel brace to the van. 'Mind how you go.'

'Thank you. Goodbye.'

They transferred the bags to the car and Nicola returned the trolley. When she re-joined Plum in the car she said, 'My mum doesn't like strange men to call her names like "love". She says it's sexist and patter-something.'

'Patronising? That's a shame, because there was a wealth of goodwill behind those little words.'

They left the wheel at a tyre-and-exhaust outlet, where the manager also addressed Plum in a way that would have caused grave offence to Nicola's mother; in fact it seemed to Plum that, well-versed though Heather was in the social sciences, she'd been careless enough to find herself in a part of the country where that kind of offence was impossible to avoid.

At home, she checked the phone for messages and found one from Nigel, which she returned.

'Nigel, welcome home.'

'Thank you, Mum.' He sounded puzzled. 'We've only been to France.'

'Nevertheless, you're still welcome. Is everyone all right?'

'Yes, fine, thank you.'

'And was the trip successful?'

'Yes, very useful. Has Nicola been behaving herself?'

'Nicola? That little tearaway?'

'What?'

'Of course she has, Nigel. She's been delightful. I imagine you'd like to speak to her? You will be kind to her, won't you?' She handed the phone to Nicola and went to put the shopping away.

Nicola came off the phone after a few minutes. She said, 'Plum, do you think it's important to find out about Uncle Hugh and Auntie Ellen?'

'It's vitally important. Why do you ask?'

'I've got to keep working and not waste time on people who are dead and gone.' Tears threatened.

'That's priceless, coming from a historian.' She drew the child towards her with her right arm and hugged her. It was becoming a habit after phone-calls from Nigel. 'There's nothing to worry about,' she said, 'because I'm going to speak to your dad very soon, but before that I'm going to give you something I always had after a difficult and disappointing time.'

'What is it?'

'I'm going to give you a comfort tea: a soft-boiled egg with toast soldiers.' She looked up at the clock. 'It's not four o'clock yet, so I don't think it will spoil dinner.'

The idea appealed to Nicola except for one detail. 'My mum doesn't call them soldiers. She doesn't like it.'

'Well no, I could have placed a substantial bet on that. What does she call them?'

' "Fingers".'

'All right. "Soldiers" is a word to be used only between these four walls.'

* * *

With the comfort tea out of the way, Plum phoned Nigel's number and got Heather.

'Nigel's out,' Heather told her. 'He shouldn't be long.'

'Good, because I have a bone to pick with him.'

'Have you?'

'Yes, and it's a big bone. It's what I believe you youngsters call an "issue", too serious for a stoppage of pocket money, more a smacking offence really.'

'Surely not.'

'But a withering telling-off may suffice. He seems to think Nicola has been wasting her time.'

'Oh yes. He wanted to know what she'd been doing, and suddenly all she could talk about was this great-aunt he'd never heard of.'

'So a great-aunt was thrust upon him. Mind you, it's probably my fault he's never heard of her. Listen, Heather, Nicola is fascinated by my Great-Uncle Hugh and also my Great-Aunt Ellen, whom she now regards as a role model. We've been looking at old letters and documents, and by studying them she's improved her reading dramatically. Do you hear what I'm saying?'

'Well yes, I suppose if it's really helping her—'

'It's filled her with enthusiasm for learning, Heather. And when I found her close to tears after speaking to Nigel I was furious. In fact I still am.'

'Oh.' Heather sounded contrite. 'Is she all right now?'

'She's quite happy. I gave her a comfort tea.'

'What did you give her?' Heather disapproved of afternoon tea and was suspicious of treats, believing that they might be either unhealthy or unethically-sourced.

'A boiled egg and toast so... cio-economic units.'

'Do you mean people?' Heather could be fussy on her own academic territory.

'Yes, tiny androgynous people, like gingerbread people or marzipan people, but made of toast.'

'All right, I get the idea.' She was quiet, and Plum wondered if she might have overdone the sardonic wit, but then her daughter-in-law said, 'Ah, that'll be Nigel now. I'll put him on.'

Plum waited. She imagined Heather would be warning him, but it would make no difference. She was no less angry when he picked up the phone.

'Mum?'

'Yes, Nigel. Now listen to me, young man....'

* * *

It was good to sit outside at the end of another warm day. Plum poured two glasses of Merlot and said, 'He actually told her she was wasting her time.'

'Oh no.'

'You know how keen she is, Paul. She was completely deflated. I spoke to her mother and she seemed to understand, although Heather's such a drip it's difficult to tell. I'm only glad we don't all have to live in Heather Land.'

The idea amused him. 'Whereabouts is it? Just so that I can avoid it.'

'Somewhere between the second star on the left and Cloud Cuckoo Land.'

'That's quite a journey. Did you get to speak to Nigel in the end?'

'Yes, I did. I told him what he'd done to Nicola, and I think he was genuinely surprised. I don't think he has a shred of imagination.'

Diplomatic as ever, Paul merely nodded.

'I insisted that he spoke to her again and put things right. It seems to have done the trick, because she was quite happy when she went to bed.'

'Good. So the search through the family archives continues with Nigel's blessing?'

'Yes, I've found several hand bills advertising recitals. Those two seem to have travelled pretty widely.'

'So their joint careers got off to a lively start.'

'It seems so, and music wasn't the only thing they got up to.' She went indoors and returned with a small newspaper cutting from The Times, which she handed to him. It was dated 3rd October 1921 and it read:

Mr H. F. Linthwaite and Miss E. W. L. Bainbridge
The engagement is announced between Hugh, third son of the late Dr and Mrs A. Linthwaite, and Ellen, only daughter of the late Mr A. Bainbridge and of Mrs E. Bainbridge, both of Cullington, Yorkshire.

'For interest's sake I've requested a copy of the marriage certificate,' she told him.

He looked puzzled. 'How did you know the date?'

'I made a guess at nineteen twenty-two. They can search a year on either side, and I think they'll come up with it. It'll be another piece of the jigsaw, and I can hardly wait.'

18

On the day after the funeral the Chairman of the School Governors announced that Colonel Pickford was unwell and might be absent for some time. He never returned, and no one knew for certain what had become of him, although various rumours circulated the common room as the weeks went by. One was that he had been appointed headmaster of an army school in Poona; another had him working at a crammer for Sandhurst candidates. Such rumours were all the same to Hugh, who was simply glad to be rid of him, and when a new headmaster was appointed he was equally disinterested. His future and Ellen's lay elsewhere. Rosen had worked hard on their behalf and secured a number of engagements, so that by October of that year they were carefully optimistic. Another aspect of their future was also constantly in their thoughts, and they discussed it as they returned by train from a recital in Manchester. They had the compartment temporarily to themselves and were able to talk freely.

'How's your mother bearing up?' Hugh had wondered from time to time but until then had been too preoccupied with the recital to ask.

'Do you mean after the shock of hearing that her only daughter is to marry an impecunious schoolmaster? She's getting used to it. I even heard her describe you to one of her friends as "a promising musician".'

'All the same, I'd rather she hadn't put that engagement notice in The Times. It's all become rather public.'

Ellen grimaced. 'Mother is old-fashioned. She likes to do things properly.' Pulling off her left glove, she held out her hand to view its latest adornment. 'She likes the ring, as well she might. It's quite beautiful.'

'Did you tell her it was my mother's?'

'Yes, and that made it respectable in her eyes. She admired your father and presumably his choice of jewellery as well.' She replaced her glove and said, 'I'm sorry to say I remember very little about him – I was a robust child – but apparently he brought me into the world. It's nice to know that, isn't it?'

'Yes, I'm certainly grateful to him for that.'

The train had been at rest for several minutes but the clashing of doors signalled that it was about to leave the station. Hugh winced when the guard blew his whistle, and then collected himself. Ellen had just asked him a question.

'I'm sorry,' he said, 'I couldn't hear you for the doors.'

'I asked you what he was like as a parent.'

He considered the question. 'He was strict but fair. He was also remarkably pragmatic for a man of his time. We were never close but he was a caring soul all the same. Just to give you an example, the second time I was wounded, and it was evident that the injury was to be of a lasting kind, he incurred considerable expense and upheaval in having a ground-floor bathroom installed.'

'The second time? I only know about the injury to your knee.'

'Oh, I had a flesh wound in nineteen-fifteen.' He touched his left upper arm. 'It healed very quickly.'

'Hugh,' she protested, 'I keep learning new things about you, and each discovery is quite alarming.'

Smiling, he reached for her hand. 'I was only wounded twice. I have no more surprises.'

'That's a relief.' Returning to the original subject, she said, 'Tell me about your mother.'

That was easier. 'My mother and I were very close; in fact I believe I was closer to her than my brothers ever were. We had a lot in common and I think that being the youngest made me special in her eyes.'

'What did you have in common?'

'Oh, people said we had similar characteristics. Also, we were both keen on music. She taught me to play the piano in the early years.' He smiled in recollection. 'You know,' he said, 'I believe she enjoyed music even more than I did.'

'Is that possible?'

'It seemed so at times. She claimed she could see sounds as well as hear them. My father called it nonsense. He said it was a figment of an over-active imagination, but she insisted that she saw a burst of colour whenever she heard a note played.'

'Imagination is a wonderful and mysterious thing.'

'And so are you. You've interrogated me about my family but I know hardly anything about yours. It's time for you to spill the beans.'

'To what?' She laughed at the absurdity of the expression.

'An American journalist I met in France used to say it.'

'All right, but it's going to be difficult. I could eulogise from now until bedtime about my nanny but I hardly knew my parents until I was grown up, and then I went to stay with my great-aunt in London, as you know. I suppose my mother is very much as you see her, and my father was always a distant sort of figure who used to send for me before bedtime and ask me about my lessons.' She looked down at her gloved hands and said, 'It's an awful thing to say, but when he died I wasn't conscious of any real loss. I suppose Edward knew him better than I did but he was killed two years before Father died, so it's anyone's guess how he might have taken it.'

To lighten the mood, Hugh said, 'But you and your nanny were close?'

'We all were: she, Edward and me. Mrs Whittaker, our cook, used to spoil us, and Hannah was forever covering up for us when we'd done something naughty.'

'I can't imagine you being naughty.'

'I told you I was the enfant terrible of the family. Be warned. Seriously, though, it seems strange that families such as mine have to rely on their servants to teach their children about love, but it was normal life as far as I was concerned until I talked with fellow-students and my violin pupils and they told me about their families.'

'There's a strange irony about privilege.'

She nodded. 'Did you know that Rose Balmforth lost her father, a brother and an uncle in the war?'

'Yes, I did.' The train entered Halifax Station and he waited until the brakes had stopped squeaking, before saying, 'I've wondered sometimes how her mother manages to buy school uniform and finance her violin lessons.'

Ellen gave a vague shrug. 'There are ways.'

'Well, it's no concern of mine.'

'No, it's not, but I was trying to tell you that Rose and her mother are devoted to each other. It's wonderful that they still have something left, and something so special, too. Have you met her mother?'

'Yes, I can't say I know her well, but Rose has the sweetest nature and she must have got that from somewhere.'

The door slid open and a couple with a suitcase entered the compartment, so Hugh and Ellen were obliged to continue their conversation when they reached Cullington.

As they climbed into a taxi, Ellen asked, 'How is your knee today?'

'Obligingly trouble-free for the time being, thank you.'

'In that case, do you think we might stop at the end of Greenacre Road and walk the rest of the way?'

'Why not? It's a fine night.' He leaned forward and repeated her request to the driver, who agreed readily, no doubt grateful for the shortened journey at that time of night.

When Hugh had paid off the taxi, Ellen took his free arm and they walked up the road past the park. 'Everyone will be in bed,' she said, 'so I can't invite you in.'

'Of course not.'

'It would be unseemly.'

'Most unseemly,' he agreed.

'Sometimes,' she said, 'I'd like to do something unseemly and let them all go to you-know-where, but I'm afraid it's out of the question.' With a glum expression, she said, 'I shan't even be able to vote until I'm thirty. That's unless they lower the voting age for women some time in the next five years, but it's unlikely.'

Feeling that he'd lost the thread of her argument, Hugh asked, 'Are you thinking of lobbying parliament to pass a law making unseemliness acceptable?'

'Not exactly, but a great many things need to be changed.'

'Agreed.'

'Where do you stand?'

'Well out of the way of politicians whenever I can. I have a very low opinion of them.'

She squeezed his arm as she so often did. 'I suppose that's not surprising, given the war and everything. I must say that my sympathies are with the Liberals, even though I was brought up in an arch-Conservative household.' She looked up at him and asked, 'Do you think Mr Asquith will ever regain power?'

'I don't know, darling. He hasn't confided in me lately.'

'Oh Hugh.' Her tone suggested that words failed her.

'Are you keen on cricket?'

'No.' It was an unequivocal and unqualified response.

'That's how I feel about party politics. Maybe one day I'll watch a cricket match and you'll attend a Liberal Party rally on the same day.'

'All right.' She patted his arm. 'We'll agree to differ.' They turned into the driveway of the house, but instead of walking up to the front door she led him to a part of the shrubbery where an unruly rhododendron afforded shelter from observation. 'There,' she said, putting her violin case down. 'No one can see us, and we can say goodnight properly.'

Surprised, he asked, 'Are you absolutely sure you haven't done this before?'

They kissed at length. So great was the luxury of seclusion after a day spent in the company of others that they held each other closely, and before long Hugh became conscious of a desire to do something very unseemly. For the time being, however, it was quite out of the question.

19

'My mum doesn't go into shops like this one,' said Nicola.

'Doesn't she?' Plum wasn't at all surprised.

'She says they malipu ....'

'Manipulate?'

'Yes, they malipulate people into spending their money.'

'Oh well, I think we're safe enough now we've done all our shopping. All that remains is to go across to Harrison's for a sticky treat. Would you like that?'

'What's Harrison's?'

'It's a coffee house and tea room, another place where they encourage extravagance, but subtly and on a more luxurious level.' She led Nicola outside and then further along the High Street until they came to a substantial stone building with a sign that read, 'Harrison's Coffee House Ltd. Est. 1912.' Plum waited for Nicola to push the door open and said, 'Prepare to be manipulated.' At that moment her attention was arrested by the reflection in the glass door of a tall, grey-haired man of sombre countenance.

'Good heavens,' she said, turning to speak to him, 'Malcolm!' She eyed the department store carrier bag in his hand and said almost theatrically, 'Have you really been shopping, and to Rimmington's of all places?'

'Hello, Plum,' he said, relaxing his air of glumness a little. 'Our wedding anniversary looms nigh and the High Street beckons accordingly.'

'Quite right.' Turning to Nicola, she said, 'Most men hate shopping, and this man is no exception. Allow me to introduce you. Malcolm, this is my granddaughter Nicola. Nicola, this is my cousin, which means he's related to you in an involved sort of way, but you'd better call him "Uncle Malcolm".' By way of further explanation, she said, 'It was his sister, Auntie Val, who gave me the desk.'

When they had asked after their respective families Plum said, 'We're about to have tea. Won't you join us?'

Malcolm hesitated and then opened the door for them. 'I'll join you in a cup of tea,' he said. 'More than that might take the edge off the appetite.'

'We must never let that happen.'

A young man came to show them to their table but Nicola was staring at a series of prints of bygone advertisements that hung on the walls.

'Come along, Nicola,' said Plum. The young man took them to a table by a window.

'The adverts on the wall....' began Nicola as the man took their coats.

'In the lobby, as we came in?'

'Yes. All the ladies had their hair done like Auntie Ellen.'

Plum nodded. 'They wore bobs. They've been popular for ever such a long time.' Turning to Malcolm, she asked, 'Are you still slaving away with the old firm?'

'I'm semi-retired now. I just look after a few long-standing clients.'

'He's an accountant,' she told Nicola. 'That's someone who does difficult sums with money and works out how much profit people have made and how much tax they owe.' She picked up the afternoon tea menu, took a quick look at it and handed it to Nicola. 'Nicola's staying with me this summer holiday,' she told Malcolm, 'to work on her arithmetic and reading and I have to say she's made tremendous progress.'

'Well done, Nicola.' Whatever difficulty Malcolm might have had in imagining such a need, he was quick to congratulate her. 'Well done, Plum as well. You're evidently a good teacher.'

'I doubt it, but I have an excellent pupil.' She took the menu and held it so that both she and Nicola could see it. 'Right,' she said, 'you could have the set tea, which is what I'm having. That's sandwiches, a scone with cream and jam and then cake of some kind. Or, you could have....' She realised that Nicola had found something on the menu that obviously appealed.

'They've got boiled eggs and toast,' said Nicola, sounding like a naturalist discovering a rare and precious species.

'Well, they're for happy occasions as well as disappointments.'

Nicola looked at her uncertainly and asked, 'Do you think they call them soldiers here, or have we to call them something different?'

Plum had already noticed a collecting box for 'Help for Heroes' beside the till. She said, 'I think they'd be surprised if you called them anything else.'

When the waitress came to take their order Plum said, 'We'd like a pot of the house blend for two, I'll have the set tea – my friend's on a diet – and... and what will you have to drink, Nicola?'

'Orange juice, please.'

The waitress wrote that down and looked at Nicola. 'And what would you like to eat, the same as your mum?'

'Can I have a boiled egg, please?'

'I think she'll probably manage a piece of cake as well,' said Plum. 'Oh, and will you cut the toast into soldiers, please?'

'Soldiers? Of course, madam.' She made a final note and left.

Nicola beamed at Plum, no doubt at being taken for her daughter again.

Malcolm asked, 'Have you found somewhere to put that old desk yet?'

'I certainly have, right next to my piano.'

'Val was relieved to be rid of it.'

'I know, but has she told you about the secret compartment?'

'What secret compartment?'

'Ah.' Plum assumed an air of mystery. 'All this time, and without anyone's knowledge, there's been a secret hiding place in that desk, containing letters and documents belonging to Uncle Hugh. Nicola and I are absolutely fascinated by it all.'

Malcolm seemed unimpressed. 'I never knew what to make of him,' he said. 'I think you knew him better than any of us. I suppose it was because you were both musicians.'

'You're forgetting my irresistible charm,' she reminded him.

'Of course.' He added guiltily, 'That goes without saying.'

'Oh, you can say it, Malcolm. I'm always ready to accept a compliment.'

The waitress made two trips to their table; the second to bring Nicola's boiled egg and toast. 'There you are,' she said like an indulgent parent, 'toast soldiers as straight as guardsmen.'

Nicola thanked her and inspected the neat stack of soldiers before breaking into her egg.

'I've been trying to find a clue or something,' said Plum, 'that might shed light on what made him so unpopular with the family.' She inspected the tea and gave it a stir before pouring it.

'I've really no idea,' said Malcolm. 'My mother, who always kept herself apart from the familial back-biting, used to say that the chief areas of contention in most family rifts were money and morals, and I daresay it was one of those two. Certainly, whatever it was caused the family to frown on them as only the Linthwaites could.' He dropped a lump of sugar into his tea and stirred it. 'They'd sit on a woolsack rather than a fence any day.'

'Don't I know it.'

Malcolm inspected the empty shell on Nicola's plate and said, 'That egg looked good, Nicola. It's what I'd have chosen.'

'It was really nice,' she confirmed.

'So what's the prognosis for your arm, Plum? We haven't spoken for ages.'

'The prognosis is the same. It's neither use nor adornment. It's been suggested that I go on playing with one hand but that's not an option as far as I'm concerned.'

'Oh? I didn't know you could do that.'

'Well, it's purely academic now.'

He nodded slowly, as if only half-understanding, and then finished his tea. 'I must go,' he said. 'I said I wouldn't be long. Thank you for the tea. We must keep in touch.' He kissed Plum's proffered cheek and said, 'It was lovely to meet you, Nicola. Keep up the good work.'

When he had gone, Nicola said, 'Uncle Malcolm's very serious, isn't he?'

'That's because he works with money. People are usually serious about money.'

'Aren't you?'

'Only when it's in short supply. Would you like to choose something from the cake trolley?' She caught the eye of a waitress, who came to the table.

'Can I have a piece of chocolate cake, please?'

'Of course.'

The waitress cut her a piece and put the plate down in front of her. Nicola thanked her.

'It's "may", not "can",' said Plum when the waitress had gone.

'Sorry.'

'Don't be. Just enjoy the cake.' She poured herself another cup of tea.

Nicola was confused, although not about grammar. She asked, 'Who sits on a woolsack?'

'What?'

'Uncle Malcolm said somebody liked sitting on a woolsack better than a fence.'

'So he did. Well, it's a tradition that the men in charge of things in the House of Lords, sort of high-up judges, sit on a woolsack. This is because of a rule that a king made hundreds of years ago, that I can't honestly remember. Anyway, when someone judges other people's behaviour we accuse them of sitting on a woolsack, just like the men in the House of Lords. It's not a real woolsack like theirs, but an imaginary one. Are you with me so far?'

'Yes.'

'But when someone won't take anyone's side in an argument we accuse them of sitting on a fence. It's an imaginary fence between the two sides, you see.'

'Right, but what has this got to do with Uncle Hugh and Auntie Ellen?'

Plum had been expecting that question. 'Certain members of our family,' she told her, 'were very quick to judge them.'

A small, elderly woman with white hair and a friendly smile had taken her place at a white-painted baby grand in the centre of the room and was thumbing through a pile of printed music.

'We're about to be entertained,' said Plum as the pianist evidently found the music she was seeking. It turned out to be a selection from *South Pacific*.

'When I was a girl,' said Plum, 'my parents sometimes brought me here, and in those days they had a trio that used to play.'

'What's a trio?'

'A trio is three people. In this case there was a violinist, a cellist and a pianist. They seemed quite elderly, and I remember that the violinist never sat with her knees together, so that her elasticated, apricot-coloured bloomers were permanently on view.'

'Ugh!'

'Mm, it was a disturbing spectacle and an unnecessary distraction, because the trio played very well.'

The pianist had come to the end of the 'Bali Hai' excerpt and was now several bars into 'Some Enchanted Evening.' Nicola asked, 'Is she playing well?'

Plum shook her head minutely. 'She's doing her best, and most of these people seem to be enjoying the music, so maybe we shouldn't be too critical.'

Her comment seemed to remind Nicola of an earlier conversation, because she asked, 'What did Auntie Ellen and Uncle Hugh do that was wrong?'

'I don't know, darling, but I'd like very much to find out.'

20

London
December 1921

'After a reception like that,' said Ellen, 'I find it hard to come down to earth. Do you mind if we don't get a taxi yet?'

'Not in the least. We could walk to the hotel. It's not far.'

'You do know what I mean, don't you?' She took Hugh's arm and they walked down Gray's Inn Road towards Acton Street. Their hotel was in Kings Cross Road. 'It's as if we're on a merry-go-round at a funfair and we have to wait for it to slow down before we can get off.'

Hugh nodded his agreement. 'That's how it seems to me.'

'What a marvellous audience they were. It was the right decision to put the César Franck at the end of the programme, wasn't it?'

'I always thought so, although Franck does have his critics, I'm told.'

'How dare they criticise him?'

He smiled at her response. 'The halls of our universities are filled with such people, and Franck is not the only object of their disapproval. He has most of the Romantic composers for company.'

'In that case, they should be confined to their halls and made to wallow endlessly in their misery. They don't deserve to hear beautiful music.'

'You're quite right.' Ellen's quixotic nature was one of her facets he loved most. 'But if we come back, and they seemed keen enough to have us, we'll need to make some changes. Maybe we could work up one of Grieg's sonatas....' He stopped when he heard raised voices ahead. Clutching his ebony cane, he said, 'I think we may take a different route.'

'What's happening?'

'There's an altercation of some kind.' Through the diffuse lamplight he made out the figure of a policeman. He appeared to be arguing with a group of men, although when they were closer Hugh saw that there were just two men, both in army uniform.

Ellen asked, 'Which way shall we go?'

'It's all right. I don't think there's a problem.'

It became clear as they approached that the policeman was apprehending the two. Hugh heard him say, 'I warned you two less than two hours ago. You've had ample time to move on.' It was this that made him decide to intervene.

'Constable, what's the problem?'

The policeman, who looked remarkably young, gave him only a cursory glance. 'There's no need for concern, sir.'

'But I am concerned. What crime have these men committed?'

'If you have to know, sir, they are loitering without visible means of support. I've moved them on once and now I'm taking them in.'

'Don't be ridiculous. These men are no danger to anyone.'

'Nevertheless, sir, under the Vagrancy Act....'

'Vagrancy poppycock!' Addressing the nearest man, who wore the stripes of a corporal on the pinned-up sleeve of his worn tunic, he asked, 'How do you men make your living?'

Perhaps recognising an influential ally, the man answered readily. 'We sing, sir. We sing songs for the public, only we've had a bad day today, sir. We came 'ere on account of there's too many busking down west, sir, an' frankly, sir, for what good we did we needn't 'ave bothered.'

Hugh read their shoulder flashes, which told him they were late of the Middlesex Regiment. 'Which battalion were you?'

'First-Eighth, sir.'

'And where did you lose your arm?'

'Second Wipers, sir.' He indicated his companion. 'We was both there, sir.'

Hugh turned to the policeman, who had been waiting with remarkable patience, and said, 'These men risked their lives fighting for their country. Where were you when this was happening?' As if on cue, his twitch returned.

The policeman remained calm. 'I was at school, sir, being too young for the army.'

'Well, all I can say is you were damned lucky. This man lost an arm in the Second Battle of Ypres, as you've heard; they both suffered untold hardships, they came home to unemployment and as if that were not enough you want to run them in because they've fallen on hard times. You should be ashamed of yourself.'

'Nevertheless, sir, they were loitering without visible means of support.'

Hugh took a one-pound note from his wallet and held it up for the policeman to see. 'Is this visible enough for you?' He pressed it into the corporal's palm. 'Is there a hostel close by?'

'There's one off Farringdon Road, sir, just round the corner from Clerkenwell Road,' the policeman told him.

'Right, lads, go and get a meal and a bed.'

The two grinned with delight. The corporal threw up a salute with his remaining arm. 'God bless you, sir. Thank you, sir.' His companion added his effusive thanks but eyed the policeman uncertainly.

'They are free to go, aren't they, Constable?'

'They are now, sir. Off you go, you two.'

The men thanked Hugh again before disappearing in the direction of Farringdon Road. Hugh felt Ellen squeeze his arm. He took it to be a gesture of support and, more importantly, it served as a recall to civility because now the men were gone he felt suddenly ashamed.

'Constable,' he said soberly, 'I shouldn't have said half those things to you. I'm afraid I get very angry when I see poverty criminalised, and especially when its victims have earned something infinitely better. Please accept my apology.'

The policeman remained as composed as ever. 'There's no harm done, sir, but it is the law of the land whether you like it or not.' He touched his helmet in salute. 'Have a good night, sir. Goodnight, madam.'

As they continued towards King's Cross Road, Hugh said, 'I'm sorry, Ellen. That was unforgivable. The man was only doing his duty, upholding the law of an ungrateful nation, one that protects the privileged, such as us, from the unpleasantness of having to witness hardship and injustice.'

'But you apologised to him, and he accepted your apology. In any case, I'm glad you helped those men. It's a disgrace that they have to make a living by singing in the streets, and it's even worse that the law is so hard on them so, good for you, I say.'

'You're loyalty itself, darling.'

'I just agree with you, and you know how those men have suffered, so it's very much to your credit that you championed their cause.'

'It's an old story, I'm afraid. You know, there was a game we sometimes played in the dugout, often when the whisky bottle had gone around a few times. The idea was that each of us had to make up an imaginary party for a trench raid. The first choice, of course, was always someone from the General Staff – Haig occupied a permanent place in it – and then we fell back on others we knew. It was the ultimate revenge on people we disliked.'

Ellen shook her head in good-natured bewilderment. 'Fascinating, darling, but what made you think of that?'

'I was only thinking how much I'd like to include that scoundrel Lloyd George in my raiding party.'

'Ah, now I understand.'

After a while Ellen said, 'We've been very fortunate, really.'

'In what way?'

'In having the Rosen agency behind us and basically getting off to such a flying start. Don't you agree?'

'Of course, although I can't help thinking that the war might have had something to do with it as well.'

Ellen hesitated momentarily in her stride. 'What on earth do you mean?'

'Only that it took its toll of a huge cross-section of society that must inevitably have included a number of musicians.'

'Are you saying that we've been successful because the war thinned out the competition?'

'Not entirely, of course, but it must have made a difference.'

'Oh Hugh.' She gripped his arm in exasperation. 'What on earth put that dismal idea into your head?'

'I'm sorry. Maybe it was meeting those two chaps tonight. I'm sorry, I shouldn't have mentioned it.'

'Oh well, I can hardly blame you in the circumstances.' She gave his arm a reassuring squeeze.

As they reached the entrance to the hotel she said, 'What you must do now is to think about the recital and the wonderful audience we had. That way you won't brood and make yourself miserable. Are you going to have a nightcap?'

'I don't think so.'

'Nor I.'

They collected their keys from the night porter and took the stairs to the first floor, where they had adjacent rooms. Ellen stopped outside hers.

'Are you going to be all right?'

'I'll be fine. Goodnight.'

'Goodnight, darling.' They kissed and parted.

Hugh sat on his bed reviewing the past hour and reviling himself for his lack of self-control. After a while he stood up to mix a powder in the hope that he might avoid a troubled night. Then, having taken his draught, he undressed and climbed into bed. Before long he felt himself drifting towards sleep.

There was a sound that was new. It made a rat-tat-tat noise, like a distant machine gun, but all gunfire had ceased, as it always did. Then, as he wrenched himself from his nightmare, he heard his name being called.

'Hugh, let me in.'

The rhythmic clatter continued and his name was called again. The voice was that of a woman.

'Hugh, darling, let me in.'

Realisation came, and he recognised Ellen's voice. She was knocking on his door. Wiping the perspiration from his eyes, he pushed the bedclothes aside and stumbled, half-awake, to the door.

There was the sound of a man's voice on the corridor, and then Ellen said something about her colleague being taken ill. The man seemed satisfied, because the next sound was of a door being closed.

Ellen slipped into the room as soon as he opened the door. 'Let me put the light on,' she said, flicking the switch. 'You must have had a terrible nightmare. I heard you through the wall.'

'I'm sorry,' he mumbled, adjusting to the light and to wakefulness itself. 'It happens sometimes. I'm sorry I disturbed you.'

'Don't be silly. Where's your dressing gown?'

'Behind the door.'

'I think,' she said, taking it from its hook, 'you'll feel much better after a bath. Have you anything to change into? I suppose that's a silly question.'

'I have a spare pair of pyjamas. I always pack them in case....'

'This happens a lot, doesn't it?'

He nodded dumbly.

'Well, don't worry on my account. I'm just concerned about you.' She helped him on with his dressing gown. 'I'll ask the night porter for some tea and I'll have it brought to my room. I think you'll find that pleasanter.'

'Thank you. I appreciate that.' He picked up his sponge bag, towel and spare pyjamas and walked down the corridor to the bathroom.

He turned on the taps and left them to fill the bath while he poured cold water into the basin and splashed it over his face until his head was clear. Then, avoiding his haggard reflection in the mirror, he moved away from the basin and tested the temperature of the bath water. It was hardly as warm as he would have liked but luxury wasn't his current priority so he made the best of what was immediately available.

When he was dried he made his way to Ellen's room, and he had to agree that it was much pleasanter than returning immediately to his with its inevitable association. He had just one misgiving.

'I feel terribly guilty,' he said, 'keeping you out of bed at....' He peered at the bedside clock.

'It's almost two o'clock, and this is a new experience for me. Don't forget I never went to school, so the clandestine midnight feasts my brother told me about were an exotic fantasy for me until now.' She patted the place beside her on the bed hospitably and poured him a cup of tea. 'But seriously, would you like to tell me about those awful nightmares?'

He put the cup to his lips and was about to sip, but he remembered a previous conversation and left it to cool for a little longer. 'I've told you more than I've told anyone about the war,' he said. 'Let's just say I'm frequently tormented about something that was neither my fault nor, for that matter, the fault of any infantry officer serving at the Front.'

'So tell me.'

'Not tonight.'

'All right,' she agreed, 'we'll just drink tea and think of happier things.'

'Our families would be horrified if they knew we were together like this. They've already condemned us for travelling together.'

'It's just as well they don't know.' She smiled easily, as if she regarded her family's disapproval as one of life's normal hazards. 'More tea?'

He looked guiltily at his empty cup. 'I've done it again, haven't I?'

'Don't worry, there are worse habits.'

'I hope there are, but I won't, thank you. I feel much better after just one.'

'You know,' she said, laying her head against his shoulder, 'I shouldn't persist, particularly in such a personal matter, but I really think it would be good for you to tell me about those horrible dreams. I mean, considering our future status. Don't you agree?'

He nodded minutely. 'When I can describe them in the cold light of day, yes, I'll tell you about them.'

'Good, because I like to think you'll confide in me when we're married.'

He raised an eyebrow. 'Is "confiding" included in the marriage vows?'

'Not in so many words.'

'It's only one word.'

'I think there's a word that covers a few things, including that.'

'In that case it seems I must.' He considered the obligation for a moment and said, 'And you want me to make an early start?'

'A sort of rehearsal, yes.' She detected a tremor as she held his arm, and said, 'Hugh, don't laugh. It's a serious matter.'

'I was only thinking that when we're not rehearsing one thing, we're rehearsing another.'

'Quite right too.'

He stroked her cheek with the backs of his fingers, delighting in the smooth softness of her skin, so that she turned her face to his and they kissed, softly at first but then with growing eagerness. Her closeness excited him, as it always did, and he gently loosened her sash to trace the curves of her body through her silk nightgown. Surprisingly, she made no protest but her breath quickened in anticipation.

Suddenly he stopped, inhibited by a return of conscience.

'We shouldn't… I mean, I shouldn't,' he said, breaking away from her. 'This is just fanning flames that are better….'

'Left unfanned? You're too noble, darling.'

'But….'

'It was going to happen eventually, so why not?'

'Perhaps we should have a rehearsal,' he agreed.

21

Nicola was with Paul, learning how to do clever things with photographs on his computer. It was a time for Plum to be alone with her thoughts, and to do that she had driven to Greenacre Road in Cullington. It was the road that skirted the north side of the park.

She knew Uncle Hugh's house because she'd visited him there in nineteen seventy-two. It was shortly before his death, although she couldn't have realised that at the time. She remembered the year, not simply because of his passing, although that was certainly significant in her life, but because it was also a time of crisis for her. Most dates, she imagined, were memorable for good or bad reasons. No one remembered the uneventful years. For the present, though, she wanted to concentrate on Uncle Hugh as he was then, and she recalled him quite easily. She remembered a smartly-dressed man with a neat moustache. 'Dapper' was the word people used at one time to describe men like Uncle Hugh, but that didn't really do him justice. A better description of his appearance would be 'soldierly.' He was, many years on, still an officer and a gentleman. And he was certainly gentle. Plum remembered feeling cared-for in his company at a time when she most needed someone to care.

Close by, an elderly man had stopped to sit on one of the benches at the edge of the green. He had walked up the road as if from the town, and now looked as if he needed to rest. Plum watched him catch his breath and asked, 'Are you all right?'

'Yes,' he said. 'Thank you for asking. I just need a bit of a breather now and then.'

'I've got my car here if you need a lift.'

He smiled and shook his head. 'No thanks, love, I'll be all right.' He looked at her inquiringly and said, 'You're not from round here, are you?'

'I am, actually, but I lived in London for many years. I came back to my roots a few months ago. I live in Welsden.'

'Welsden? That's a grand place to live. I live just down the hill.' He pointed in the direction from which he had come. 'Moffatt Lane.' He laughed. 'It sounds like the little lass in that nursery rhyme, doesn't it? It's just spelled different.'

Plum decided she liked the old man.

'We used to come up here courting,' he told her, 'me and my wife.' He added, 'Before we were wed.'

'Of course.'

He seemed to dwell on that reminiscence before saying, 'You seem to be interested in the doctor's house.'

'I beg your pardon?'

'That's what we used to call it. I don't remember the doctor myself, of course. I believe he passed away in the flu epidemic at the end of the First World War, but that's what everybody called it. You know how names tend to stick long after they've given up having any meaning.' He nodded philosophically. 'It's student accommodation now, like most of the big houses in the area.'

'My great-uncle lived there.'

'Did he?' The man pondered for a minute, possibly absorbed in the necessary arithmetic, and then he asked, 'Do you mean Mr Linthwaite?'

'Yes, did you know him?'

'Everybody knew him. Mr and Mrs Linthwaite were what you'd call respected figures in the neighbourhood. He was a much-decorated man in the First World War, you know.'

'Yes, I know.'

'My dad was in his company and he always said there was no finer officer.' He reflected on that accolade and added, 'We could have done with a few like him in the last war instead of some of the daft buggers we were lumbered with.' He turned to Plum apologetically and said, 'Pardon my French, love.'

'That's all right. You were in the war, then?'

'At the end of it, really. They posted me to Germany first, and then to Palestine. That were a right old mess, and they still haven't sorted it out.'

'That's true.'

'I'll tell you something I remember about Mr and Mrs Linthwaite.' The old man leaned towards her confidingly. 'My sister and I used to come up here to listen to them playing. You know he played the piano, don't you? And she played the violin. She didn't work under her married name – she was always billed as Ellen Bainbridge – but she was married to him all right. Anyway, we used to stand outside the house and listen to them playing. It was glorious. Sometimes we got so caught up in the music we forgot the time and then we got into bother when we were late home, but it was worth it. We were both keen on music, you see, but there was no money at our house for lessons.' He grinned cheekily and said, 'We always said that folk paid good money to hear Mr and Mrs Linthwaite, and we got to hear 'em for nowt.'

'Did you ever meet them?'

'Aye, we did. When the lady who used to look after them got married again and left their employment – she'd been a widow, you see – they didn't take on anybody new, and we used to run errands for them. They were generous too, and Mrs Linthwaite, you know, was a lovely person. She was a lady, of course, one of the Bainbridge family that was part of Adams and Bainbridge the wool merchants. They got taken over at one time by one of them big conglomerates but the name Adams and Bainbridge survived. It's a shame these people can't leave well alone,' he reflected. 'It's greed, that's all it is.'

Plum looked at her watch. It was a little before eleven. 'Look,' she said, 'I usually have a cup of coffee at about this time. Is there somewhere around here where we can get one?'

'There's the van,' he said, pointing to a white trailer parked about a hundred yards up the road. A painted sign identified it as 'Kev's Diner.' Plum had seen it but taken little notice until then. It would be a new experience for her. She asked, 'Can I offer you a cup of coffee or something?'

'A cup of tea would be champion, thank you.'

'Very good.' She lent him her right hand. 'I'd bring your tea down to you but I've only one arm that works.'

'Oh, that's no good, is it?' He rose to his feet and together they set off towards the diner.

'By the way,' said Plum, 'I'm Victoria Harvey. That's my married name but I'm actually a Linthwaite.' She offered her hand, which he took.

'I'm Stanley Goldthorpe,' he said, 'and I'm pleased to meet you.' When they'd walked a few more steps he said, 'If you don't mind my asking, how did your arm come to be like that?'

'It was injured in an accident a couple of years ago. The driver of an articulated lorry pulled out without seeing us. My husband was killed and I was left with very little use in my left arm.'

'I'm sorry to hear that, love. What a terrible thing to happen.'

'It certainly was. I lost my livelihood as well.'

'Dear, oh dear. What did you used to do?'

'The same as my great-uncle, I was a pianist.'

He stopped, as if he were unable to walk and show sympathy at the same time. 'Really? You lost all that, and with so much of your life before you.'

'I was sixty at the time.'

'That's what I mean. You were no more than a lass.'

She smiled. It was good to be 'no more than a lass,' if only in the eyes of an old man.

They reached the diner, where one customer was being served. When their turn came Plum looked up at the huge man behind the counter. He was clad in jeans and a T-shirt, and his neck and arms were covered in tattoos. She said, 'Tea, please, and I'd like an Americano if that's possible.'

The man smiled good-naturedly and said, 'I can do you an instant coffee, love, and when you've paid for it you can call it what you like.' He poured tea and coffee into plastic beakers and pointed to a jug of milk and a bowl of sugar. 'Help yourselves,' he said.

'Thank you.' She handed over three pounds. 'Mr Goldthorpe, would you like to do your own milk and sugar?' She watched him shovel a remarkable quantity of sugar into his tea and then added milk to her coffee. She thanked Kev, whose name was printed conveniently on his T-shirt, and joined Mr Goldthorpe on a bench nearby.

'It's my knees,' he explained. 'They're not very forgiving.'

'You're right to rest them.'

'I come up here most days,' he told her. 'It's a good job these benches are here 'cause I have to walk from one to t' next, but I won't let it beat me.'

'Quite right.' She had to ask, 'Why do you come here?'

''Cause this is where we did our courting, like I told you.'

'I see. How long have you been on your own?'

'Ten years, three months and... a few days.'

'It's not easy, is it?'

'No, well, you know what it's like.'

'Yes.' It seemed to her that she was coping with widowhood rather better than Mr Goldthorpe was. It was maybe time to change the subject. She asked, 'Do you know where the Bainbridge family lived?'

'Oh, them.' He thought for a moment and said, 'They say the old lady lived in the big house, number one-hundred-and-fifty.' He pointed beyond the trailer to a house set apart from the rest. 'It's a place for teachers to go on courses now, so my daughter tells me. Mind you, I think they only go there to have a rest from the kids, and I can't say as I blame them for that.'

The coffee was awful, and Plum was just throwing the remainder of it over the grass, when Mr Goldthorpe said, 'You know, nice as Mr and Mrs Linthwaite were, there were always rumours about family quarrels and upsets, but I imagine you'll know more about that than I do.'

'I only wish I did.'

He threw his plastic beaker into the waste bin beside the bench. 'Well,' he said, 'you know what families can be like.'

'Yes, I know only too well, and the greatest sadness is that those two never had children.'

'No, they'd no kids, at least as far as I'm aware.'

22

February 1922

'You have the interest here, Ellen.'
'What?'
'The four bars beginning at one-oh-five. You have the theme, and I think you need to bring it out more.'
'I'm sorry.'
'Let's go from bar ninety-six.' They began again, but before long it was obvious to Hugh that Ellen's concentration was elsewhere. He stopped again. 'What's the matter, darling?'
'Mm?'
'Something's on your mind and it's certainly not the music.'
She sighed heavily. 'Oh dear. Perhaps we should sit down and talk.'
'By all means.' He waved her to the sofa.
She sat down and waited for him to join her. Then she took a deliberate breath and said, 'You know, don't you, that since that night in London I've been using a device to avoid becoming pregnant?'
'Yes.' The nature of the thing was a mystery to him but he knew that Ellen had visited a clinic in London, where she'd obtained the equipment along with a quantity of advice.
She bit her lip. 'It turns out I needn't have been in such a hurry to make that arrangement. The damage was already done.'

Suddenly, he felt empty. 'That first time?' He'd detected an element of passive reluctance on her part of late and wondered if something was troubling her, but the possibility of pregnancy hadn't occurred to him.

'Yes, I fondly imagined that being a virgin meant I wouldn't conceive. Apparently that's a popular fallacy, although I must say its popularity has faded somewhat recently, at least from my point of view.'

A piece of half-burned coal fell against the grate and Hugh glanced irritably at the fire, resenting the distraction. 'How long have you known?'

'It's been eight weeks since my last monthly event. I suppose I began worrying after the fourth week.' She added, 'It's always occurred with metronomic regularity.'

'I see, and you've had it confirmed?'

She nodded miserably.

'Well, as I see it, there's only one thing to be done.'

She lowered her eyes. 'I couldn't face going to, you know, one of those people.'

'And I wouldn't hear of it. I meant that we must bring our wedding day forward.'

Relief gave way to uncertainty. 'I haven't announced it yet.'

'Good, it means you don't have to change anything. No one will be any the wiser.'

'They won't until they count the months between our wedding and the birth of the baby. Anything less than nine will set tongues wagging as never before.'

'Yes, the world is full of malicious mathematicians.'

'My family certainly is.'

'And mine.'

Wheels were turning furiously in Hugh's mind as he speculated on how they might minimise the damage. Eventually he said, 'Let's confound them.'

'How?'

'By treating it as the joyful affair it really is. You and I are going to be parents and we're going to do it in a way that people will notice.' His enthusiasm continued to burgeon as he developed the theme. 'Ours will be no ordinary child; it will have parents who are loving, sensitive, dedicated, ambitious, intellectual, analytical, intuitive, philosophical and, above all, blessed with talent. Inside your slender frame Little Ellen or Tiny Hugh – I don't care which – may, at this very moment, be deciding between the violin and the piano. My advice, of course, will be to learn both, at least; the greater the array of options the more rewarding the choice can be, but we can deal with that in due course. Meanwhile, I suggest we celebrate with a drink. What will you have?'

Ellen closed her eyes in bewilderment. 'Hugh, you've just transformed a catastrophe into a cause for celebration, and that is a great deal for me to take in all at once. Give me a moment, please.'

'Very well.' He looked up at the mantel clock. 'Your moment is up. Would a glass of sherry be acceptable?'

'Highly acceptable, thank you.'

He took two glasses and plied the sherry decanter generously. 'Yours, my love,' he said, handing a glass to her with as much of a flourish as he could manage without spilling the sherry. 'Let's drink to "The Next Linthwaite".'

Ellen joined him in the toast a little less boisterously and then said, 'I'm afraid you're forgetting something.'

'What am I forgetting?'

'I hate to place a damper on this extraordinary celebration, but we have to take into account the arrangements.'

'What arrangements?'

'The arrangements my mother wants to make, which clash inevitably with those my aunts and uncles have in mind. The only detail on which they're agreed is that it should be a lavish wedding and that will inevitably take time to organise.' She took an unmaidenly draught of sherry for fortification. 'And not to put too fine a point on it, time is not plentiful.'

'It's not, I agree.' Hugh was thinking. It was too bad that all those family members wanted to dictate the wedding arrangements, and it was even worse that the last people to be consulted were the two about to be wed. 'I know,' he said, draining his glass and refilling it, 'we'll steal a march on them all.'

Ellen had yet to be enthused. 'What are you talking about, darling?'

'Let's arrange our own wedding.'

'Do you mean secretly?'

'Yes, let's do the whole thing covertly, the arrangements and the ceremony itself, and then present our newly-married status as a fait accompli. Then, if there's any argy-bargy—'

'Oh, there'll be plenty of that.'

'We can tell them we did it because we were sick to death of their eternal bickering, not to mention their interference in our lives.'

'And spring the pregnancy on them later?'

'Yes, let's not allow them too much ammunition in the opening skirmish.'

She looked slowly into her glass, at the clock, at the fire and then at him. 'You're completely mad,' she said, 'but you've convinced me. It's the only way.'

'It is,' he agreed. 'We must find out about a licence and all that kind of thing, and then we can act.' He added boyishly, 'Forward, the Fourteenth!'

'This predicament is the result of someone being a little too forward, wouldn't you say?' She checked herself. 'No, that's not fair. I was equally to blame, perhaps more so than you.'

'Let's not talk about blame. Let's just take the credit.'

His dogged optimism made her smile. 'It's impossible to look on the dark side for long when I'm with you.'

'My whole outlook was pretty dark before I met you,' he told her soberly, 'and you must take the credit for changing that.'

23

Plum wasn't really listening to Nigel. She could see his mouth opening and closing – at least, she thought she could, because his whiskers were well overdue for a trim – but the words made no sense. She was actually thinking about her meeting on the park with Mr Goldthorpe, and that was wrong of her, because she'd invited Nigel, Heather and Matthew over and was failing in her duty as hostess. Matthew had gone into the garden. Presumably he was no more riveted by revelations from the battlefields of northern France than she was.

She wondered idly if Nigel might look less stern without his beard and moustache, but he'd had them so long it was difficult to say. She forced herself to concentrate on what he was saying.

'The Battles of Azincourt and Dien Bien Phu were fought more than five hundred years apart but the similarities are quite striking. For one thing, they were both fought around three fortifications, each of which fell in turn.'

'Really, dear? If only the French had realised that.'

'Unfortunately, "if only" has no place in history.'

'That's very sad, but situations, consequences and even lives can be changed.'

'They frequently are, but what I'm saying is that it's not the historian's province to conjecture on what might have been.' He appeared to be glaring again but it was probably a combination of the severe glasses and unruly facial hair. They gave altogether the wrong impression.

'On the other hand it is within his remit in this case to listen to his mother, who would like very much to tell him about his daughter's progress.'

'Oh, yes.' He relaxed the stern look a little. 'I gather she knows all her tables now.'

'And much more than that, but wouldn't it be better if we asked Nicola to tell you what she's been doing?'

On hearing her name, Nicola looked up from her book.

Plum held out her arm and asked, 'Would you like to read something aloud to your mum and dad, Nicola?'

'Okay.' She got up from the floor and stood beside Plum's chair, seemingly unsure how to proceed.

'You could read the page you've just read to yourself,' Plum suggested.

Self-consciously, Nicola began.

' "There on the floor was Amanda's pen, the one she thought she'd lost. Clarissa knew it was Amanda's by its black-and-gold zig-zag pattern. No one else had one like it.

' "Suddenly she had an idea. She would put it in Jane's bag when she wasn't looking. Jane was easily the most unpopular girl in the house or, if it came to that, in the whole school, and if Miss Thornton thought she'd stolen the pen she would be in big trouble." '

She stopped reading, having reached the end of the page. Plum noticed the illustration that covered almost half the page, and imagined Nicola would be thankful for it. It must have been quite an ordeal.

Nigel nodded approvingly. 'Well done, Nicola,' he said.

'I'm not sure about the reading matter,' said Heather.

'But you are prepared to congratulate your daughter on her progress?' Plum was determined to extract a hearty word of praise from her somehow.

'Yes, I just wonder why she has to read stories about girls from privileged backgrounds.'

'Rather than simply pretending they don't exist, like haemorrhoids or thrush?' Not for the first time, Plum was thankful that politics left her unmoved.

'There's no need to be facetious. I simply question the need for books that teach middle-class values to impressionable children.'

'Go on, Heather, say it. You know you want to. Tell Nicola how wonderfully well she's done. We're all behind you.' She leaned forward encouragingly.

'Well, of course. Well done, Nicola.'

'I'm sure you realise how much that means to her.' Plum hoped she did. Meanwhile, she had another surprise. 'We've also been learning some social history,' she told them. Having seized both Nigel's and Heather's attention, she said, 'We spent a useful afternoon at Cullington Folk Museum, and now Nicola can tell you about life in a working-class home in the nineteen-twenties.' She gave Nicola's arm a squeeze and said, 'Tell them about how they washed their clothes, Nicola.'

'Oh, yes.' For some reason the subject had particular appeal for her. 'They didn't have washing machines,' she told her parents,' so they put soap on the clothes and rubbed them on a wash board and they heated the water in a boiler and poured it into a peggy tub with a piggin and then they possed it with a posser 'til it was clean. Then they rinsed it and got the water out by hand with a mangle and then they hung it on a creel over the fire to dry, and when it was dry they ironed it. They had to heat the iron on the hob in front of the fire, and then it was time to cook dinner, and when that was all over they were ready for bed but the hard work didn't end—'

'Good girl. I think we'll leave it there.'

Nicola gave her an indignant look. 'No, they had to wash the dishes after dinner. That was before they could go to bed.'

'Well I never,' said Heather, possibly conscious that she was still under scrutiny. 'You certainly learned a lot.'

'Yes,' said Nigel, 'It was a very comprehensive description.'

Plum groaned inwardly. 'History's very demanding, isn't it, Nigel?'

'It's only like any other discipline. At all events, she'll have a lot to talk about when she goes back to school.'

'Back to school in two weeks,' said Matthew, coming in from the garden. 'It would be all right if I had the right equipment.' He was a serious boy of sixteen, keen to get to grips with 'A' Levels.

'Matthew's dissatisfied,' Heather told her, 'because we won't buy him the scientific calculator he wants. He's already had new trainers and a notepad this summer, and he has to learn that we can't just wave a magic wand and make the money appear.'

'It would be an investment, Mum,' Matthew assured her. 'It does non-symbolic integration and differentiation.'

'The answer is still "no".'

It sounded to Plum like the kind of monster no civilised person would allow indoors but she nevertheless asked him, 'What does this thing cost, Matthew?'

'Fifteen quid.'

'You'll have to save up,' Nigel told him.

'I asked,' said Plum, because I've already given Nicola quite a lot, so how would it be if I paid for the calculator?'

There was a brief but silent conversation between the two parents, involving a degree of eyebrow twitching, before Nigel said, 'If you want to do that, Mum, go ahead.'

Matthew was suddenly and unusually animated. 'Thanks, Gran. That's great!'

' "Plum",' she reminded him. Then, noticing that Nicola was temporarily out of the room, she said, 'I've been meaning to speak to you about something else.'

'Oh?' Nigel was looking stern again. She wished he wouldn't.

'Would either of you have any objection if I took Nicola for a haircut?'

They both looked blank.

'You see, she's mentioned on a couple of occasions that she'd really like her hair cut in a bob.'

Heather said, 'I've never encouraged her to regard that sort of thing as important.'

'I know.' Plum thought of the child's uneven, overgrown fringe and split ends that looked as if they'd been trimmed with garden shears and, now she looked more closely, Heather's hair was no better. 'It has nothing to do with vanity,' she explained. 'It's about feeling good about herself. For my money that's what's been holding her back at school, and it would make such a difference to her.'

'Well,' said Heather, 'if you put it like that, I don't suppose it'll do any harm. In the normal way I might have been inclined to object.'

Before she could say more on the subject of material values the phone rang and as he was closest to it Nigel picked it up.

He seemed to be exchanging pleasantries with someone he knew but hadn't seen for some time. It was impossible to tell who the caller was, until he handed the phone to Plum and said, 'It's Uncle Malcolm, Mum.'

She took the phone from him. 'Hello Malcolm.'

'Hello Plum. How nice to have the family to visit.'

'Yes, it should happen more often.'

Typically, Malcolm came straight to the reason for his call. 'Actually, I was thinking about our conversation in Harrison's, you know, about Uncle Hugh and the family, and something came back to me that I'd completely forgotten.'

'I'm all ears.'

'Well, I remember trying to piece things together once, long ago, and I asked my father if Aunt Ellen was Uncle Hugh's wife. I was very young and confused, and I don't know how the subject came up, but I do remember his answer. He said, "Yes, if you can call them married, and I certainly don't call what they had a marriage." He was quiet for a while, brooding, you know, and then he said something like, "And to go off and do it with her mother on her death-bed, well, that was the limit. I shan't tell you what else they got up to because, mercifully, you're too young to understand." Now, those may not have been his exact words – it's impossible to remember every detail after so many years – but that's basically what he said.'

24

'I love you, Mrs Linthwaite.'

'Well now, there's a coincidence, Mr Linthwaite, because I love you too.' She settled herself down more snugly with her head against Hugh's chest and said, 'You know what we're doing, don't you?'

'Yes, we're luxuriating in the aftermath of our first officially-sanctioned spot of you-know-what.'

'You make it sound like something that happens in one of those wretched countries where no one has any rights and the state dictates everything.'

'I imagine they encourage people to do it all the time in Russia, at least in wintertime. By all accounts it's the only way they can keep warm.'

'Well, it's too good for the horrible people who murdered the Tsar and his family. I hope they never know pleasure again.' She lifted her head to ask, 'How did we get on to this subject?'

'You asked me if I knew what we were doing.'

'Oh yes, I'm just saying that in a self-indulgent way all we're doing is postponing the evil moment when we have to face my mother.'

He looked shocked. 'Is that why you came back with me?'

'No, I came because you insisted on consummating the marriage, even though we've consummated it many times before.'

'Those other times don't count.' He added, 'Legally speaking, that is.'

She raised her head to view him through half-closed eyes. 'You just wanted to have your way with me in the middle of the afternoon. I've heard about roués like you.' She looked up again. 'Why is it never in the morning?'

'Because Mrs Naylor is here most mornings.'

'That would certainly present an obstacle.' She ran her fingers idly through the hairs on his chest and said, 'Tell me about Mr and Mrs Knowles. We never really had a proper conversation with them.'

'Yes, it's a pity they had a train to catch. When I asked them to be witnesses they'd already arranged their journey and they only agreed to do it when I told them the appointment was for nine-thirty.'

'That was a stroke of luck. You knew him in the army, didn't you?'

'Henry was in my company. We were wounded in the same assault.'

'Yes, he has quite a limp.'

He gave her an odd look. 'That's because he has only one leg.'

'Oh, I didn't realise.'

'You weren't to know. It's not the kind of thing a chap tells you when he turns up to witness a clandestine marriage. I suppose I should have mentioned it to you before we met them.'

'Oh well, you couldn't think of everything, and it was good of them to do what they did.' As an afterthought, she said, 'I don't suppose it was much of a coincidence that you and he were wounded at the same time.'

'No, it certainly wasn't. All the officers in the battalion who weren't killed on the Ridge were wounded.'

'Really? That's horrible.'

'It certainly was.' Suddenly he brightened. 'But it turned out well in the end for Henry and me. He met Beatrice in a military hospital, and you befriended me, if you remember, when my knee let me down outside Harrison's Coffee House.'

'How could I forget standing in the rain and yelling like a fishwife for the policeman to come and help me?'

'Yes, I remember admiring your projection. I wondered at the time if you'd had singing lessons.'

She supported herself on one elbow and said, 'I suppose one of us should place a notice in The Times.'

'I've taken care of that.'

'What an organised and efficient eloper you are. What will it say?'

'I think I asked them to print, "Hugh Linthwaite and Ellen Bainbridge announce their marriage at Bradford Registry Office on the fourth of March nineteen-twenty-two," or something like that. It should appear on Monday.'

'And then the fun will begin.'

'What can they do? We're both free and of marrying age. In any case, it'll be a nine-day wonder.'

She shook her head firmly. 'Scandals last a lifetime, and sometimes even longer.' She rolled over to glance at the clock. 'It's nearly three,' she said, 'and we can't put it off much longer. We must go and break the news.'

* * *

They opened the front door and found Hannah the maid waiting, distraught and with red-rimmed eyes.

'Miss Ellen,' she said, 'I didn't know where you were so I couldn't telephone you.'

'What on earth's the matter, Hannah?'

'It's Mrs Bainbridge, Miss Ellen. I found her when I came to tell her lunch was served. I found her collapsed in her armchair. I sent for the doctor and he came straight away but it was too late.' She lowered her voice. 'I'm sorry, Miss Ellen.'

25

There were three letters in the same hand. One was addressed to Miss E. Bainbridge at 150 Greenacre Road, and the other two were addressed to Mr and Mrs Linthwaite but the envelopes were not addressed. They'd obviously been delivered by hand. Plum took out the letter addressed to Miss E. Bainbridge. It was dated 7th March 1922 and was written in a girlish hand but in a mature style.

Dear Miss Bainbridge,
I am very sorry indeed to hear of your loss….

It said basically what Plum would expect a letter of condolence to say. That was until the final paragraph.

So as not to intrude on you at this time I will not expect a lesson until I hear from you.
Yours, with much sympathy,
Rose Balmforth.

Rose Balmforth was presumably a violin pupil, possibly a child whose parent had helped her with the letter. At all events, it was evident that she was fond of her teacher.

She opened the next, which was dated 14th March. Its style was less mature than the first but the sentiments expressed in it sounded equally sincere.

Dear Mr and Mrs Linthwaite,
I want to be the first to congratulate you both and wish you happiness. I know the news of your wedding has come at a difficult time, so soon after your sad loss, but when I heard that my two favourite teachers had got married I was very happy, and I still am.
Yours, with very best wishes for a happy future together,
Rose.

The absence of dates was tantalising. If only the copy marriage certificate would arrive. Plum had paid for the Standard Service but, even allowing for that, the thing was due to arrive in the post any time. Fortunately, she had opted for the Priority Service when she requested a copy of Mrs Bainbridge's death certificate, so it could also arrive soon. Unfortunately, she had no idea whether or not the death certificate would give the time of death. Tom's certificate showed only the date.

She opened the third letter, dated 28th April, and found no reference to either event. Instead, the child had news of her own.

Dear Mr and Mrs Linthwaite,
I learned today that the Royal Manchester College of Music have awarded me the scholarship! I simply cannot believe my luck, and I owe so much to both of you. I owe it to Mrs Linthwaite for her excellent teaching, her kindness, generosity and inspiration, and to Mr Linthwaite for all his encouragement and helping me through Higher School Certificate. I miss him now that he is no longer at the Grammar School. I am also very grateful indeed to Mrs Linthwaite for arranging the Adams and Bainbridge Bursary. Without that I would not be able to take up the scholarship. Thank you again. I will do my best to make you both proud of me.
Yours sincerely,
Rose.

Plum recalled her joy on hearing about her scholarship in 1969, and felt a kind of kinship with the girl, who must have been seventeen or maybe eighteen, and who had felt the same elation she had at that age. Plum had another link with the girl as well; she still had the letter Uncle Hugh had written to her, congratulating her on her success. She would look that out later. Meanwhile she continued to search the contents of the secret compartment. There were envelopes there that she remembered leaving until later, when something of immediate interest had captured her notice, and she would certainly examine them when she had completed her rummage. There were also some photographs that might turn out to be interesting, although not for the time being. She picked her way through each item more meticulously than ever before, until she found a tiny newspaper cutting. It was from the Births, Marriages and Deaths column of The Times, and she gave a little cry of delight. It was the notice of Uncle Hugh and Aunt Ellen's wedding, which had apparently taken place at Bradford City Registry Office on 4th March 1922.

'I hear excited sounds from within.' It was Paul's voice from the kitchen.'

'Come in, Paul. I've just turned up more information.'

'Important information, by the sound of it.' He sat beside her on the sofa.

'You must think I'm out of my mind, doing all this.'

'Not at all. It never occurred to me; in fact I look forward to hearing about each revelation as it happens.'

Having decided that he was quite serious, she said, 'I've been reading these letters. They're from a girl at Uncle Hugh's school, who was one of Aunt Ellen's violin pupils.' As she handed him the letters it occurred to her that the house was remarkably quiet. 'I wonder where Nicola is,' she said.

'She's round at my place with Abbey and Tamsin. They don't play nowadays; they're "hanging out".'

'Hopefully not pegged to a clothes line.'

'That's just what I thought.' He read the letters and handed them back. 'She must have been rather special,' he said, 'not just talented but a nice kid as well.'

Plum nodded. 'The kind you never forget.' She showed him the marriage notice. 'Does anything about this strike you as odd?'

'Bradford Registry Office,' he mused. 'If they lived in Cullington, why did they get married in Bradford? It's also interesting that they chose a registry office wedding. I'm surprised an old family like the Bainbridges would do that.'

'Unless the couple arranged the marriage independently of their families for whatever reason, and did the deed in Bradford to keep it absolutely to themselves.'

'The trouble is,' said Paul, looking idly through the pile that Plum had been sifting, 'there's a danger of reading too much into their actions. They were obviously out on a limb, at least where his family were concerned, but we shouldn't conjecture.'

'We shouldn't, but there's one possibility that would fit, and that is that a quick and clandestine marriage was very necessary.'

'Do you mean they might have rung the bus off before the driver was in his seat?'

'That's a quaint way of putting it, Paul, but yes, she may have been pregnant. To put it another way, Uncle Hugh may have started a family tradition.'

'Really?'

'Yes, I made my contribution in nineteen seventy-two, when I became pregnant with Nigel and had to marry his father.'

Paul's face was expressionless. 'I'd no idea,' he said, 'not that it makes any difference to anything. All the same, though, it must have been a very bad time for you.'

'It was the second-worst time of my life,' she confirmed, 'the absolute worst being the accident.' She added, 'I'll tell you about it sometime but you'll find it hard to believe.'

'Would you believe I've just found another piece of the puzzle?' He gave her a dog-eared and twice-folded sheet of paper that he'd found in the pile.

'Good heavens.' She scanned the document quickly but the main body of it was of little interest to her. It was an information sheet from Bradford Registry Office, basically a reminder list and briefing for the intending couple, but of far more importance was a handwritten note in the top right-hand corner, which said, *4th March, 9:30 a.m.*

'Well,' said Paul, 'at least you know the time of the wedding. All you have to do now is find out the circumstances of Mrs Bainbridge's death.'

'That's all,' she agreed.

26

'It happened at one o'clock,' said Ellen, 'while we were celebrating, and that's awful, although I feel most guilty about Hannah. Just imagine the poor woman waiting for me all that time.'

'Nothing you or I did was at all callous or even careless. There's no need to feel guilty about anything, although I suppose you inevitably will.'

'Yes, you know all about irrational guilt, don't you? I'm thinking of those awful nightmares of yours.' Suddenly she started anxiously. 'The notice,' she said, 'in the newspaper, it'll be in Monday's Times.'

'No, it won't. I phoned them while you were with your mother. They're going to hold it back for another week. I couldn't realistically make it longer than that.'

'No,' she agreed, 'we'll be damned for being married on the day she died or for announcing the marriage too close to the funeral, which, incidentally, I have to arrange, never having arranged one before.'

'The undertaker will guide you through it,' he assured her, 'and I'll be with you as well. I arranged both my parents' funerals.'

'Hugh,' she said, laying her hand on his, 'you're the best support anyone could wish for. When I'm weak and feeble you brace me up.' She appeared to reflect on that momentarily and said, 'Maybe I'm not being weak and feeble enough. I feel guilty now because the initial shock has receded and I haven't gone completely to pieces. Is one supposed to feel like this on losing a parent?'

'I think that depends on the relationship you had with your parent.'

'She didn't go out of her way to be popular,' she agreed, reaching for the bell.

Less than a minute later Hannah entered the room. 'Yes, Miss Ellen?' She was composed and no longer looked tearful.

'Hannah, will you ask Mrs Whittaker to come and see me. I'd like to speak to you both.'

'Yes, Miss Ellen.'

When the door was closed behind her, Hugh asked, 'What are you going to say to them?'

'I'm going to tell them we're married.'

'Do you think that's wise?'

'I think so. I grew up with those two in the house and I'd feel guiltier if I kept them in the dark than I would if I never told my family.'

'Will they be discreet?'

'They won't tell a soul. Trust me.'

The door opened and the two servants came in. Mrs Whittaker the cook, a short, grey-haired woman, regarded them unsurely.

'What I'm going to tell you,' said Ellen, 'must not go outside this room until the official announcement is made. I know I can trust you. You see, the reason I wasn't here today is that Mr Linthwaite and I were married this morning.' The servants gasped audibly, but Ellen went on. 'We did that so that we could have a simple wedding rather than have to cope with all the lavish arrangements that were being made. Now, you can imagine how I feel, knowing that my mother met her end whilst we were celebrating. We had no way of knowing it was going to happen, but it was nevertheless most unfortunate that the two things took place on the same day.' She paused for a few seconds but there was no reaction. 'People will be upset, and cross words will be said, but that need not affect either of you. I simply wanted you both to know because it's only right that, as faithful and long-serving members of this household, you should be given that courtesy. Do you understand?'

The two looked at each other awkwardly and nodded, smiling. Mrs Whittaker spoke first, as protocol dictated. 'We understand, Miss Ellen... I mean Mrs Linthwaite.'

'In view of the circumstances I think it will be safer to hold on to "Miss Ellen" for the time being, Mrs Whittaker. I'll let you know when the time comes.'

'Of course, Miss Ellen. Anyway, we'd both like to wish you and Mr Linthwaite much happiness, even at this sad time.' She added unsurely, 'I hope that makes sense.'

'It makes perfect sense, Mrs Whittaker. By the way, what are you preparing for dinner?'

'I was doing cold cuts, Miss Ellen. That's what Mrs Bainbridge wanted.' Her voice faltered. 'You know how she hated waste.'

'Yes, I do. Will you prepare that, please? And then you can both take the evening off.'

'Thank you, Miss Ellen. Thank you, sir.'

When they were gone, Ellen said, 'Those were my first instructions as mistress of the house. It's just a shame it's going to be short-lived.'

'What do you mean?'

'This house is much too big for two of us and it's very expensive to maintain. As things are, Hannah has her hands full doing the work of two, and they both want to retire. I've known that for some time.'

A minute or so after leaving the room, Hannah returned to say, 'Dr Rawnsley is on the telephone, wishing to speak to you, Miss Ellen.'

'Thank you, Hannah.' Ellen followed her out, leaving Hugh to ponder their predicament. As Ellen had pointed out, they would be damned whatever they did, so their only sensible course was to brace themselves and be prepared to stonewall if necessary.

Ellen returned very quickly. 'It was only to tell me he's bringing the death certificate tomorrow,' she said. 'He's given the cause of death as heart failure.'

'Had she a heart condition?'

'Yes, he took that into account.' She stared down at her hands, so that he asked, 'What is it?'

'Only that I should feel some measure of grief, but I feel guilty because I don't, and resentful that I should.' She looked up again. 'What happens next?'

'You have to register the death. You'll need to get several copies of the death certificate signed by the Registrar, because you'll need to send them to your mother's bankers, stock-broker, insurance companies and so on. Then he'll give you a document authorising her burial and you can make the funeral arrangements.'

She shook her head in perplexity. 'Hugh,' she said, 'what would I do without you?'

'I don't know.' He gave an awkward smile. 'All the same, for appearance's sake I think we should be discreet for the time being about our living arrangements.'

27

Plum's day began with disappointment. The copies of the marriage and death certificates arrived in the same post but the death certificate yielded little more information than she already knew. Mrs Bainbridge had apparently died of cardiac failure on the 4th March 1922 at the age of 54 years. Mr Goldthorpe had referred to her as 'the old lady,' and Plum could only imagine that fifty-four was considered fairly senior in the nineteen-twenties. The fact remained, however, that there seemed no way of establishing the time of her death, and she shared her disappointment with Paul when he came in from mowing her lawn.

'But surely you don't believe that rubbish,' he said, 'about them going off to get married while she lay gasping on her death bed?'

'Not for one minute, but I do like to have things cut and dried. The family seem to have compiled a pretty thorough dossier on them and even though it no longer matters to them I still want to put together a defence.'

'Plum,' he said, accepting a cup of coffee, 'when you first told me about this business I thought it would be an excellent thing for you, a distraction from your immediate problem, and it seems to have done that job rather well until now, but it's become much more than that, and I wonder if it's doing you more harm than good.'

'Really?' His concern surprised her.

'Yes, it's become an irritation rather than a pleasure.'

'Good heavens, Paul, what on earth gave you that idea?'

'Your frustration at not being able to nail the time of death is a reasonable clue.'

'Do you call that frustration?'

'What else can I call it?'

Plum looked far from frustrated. 'Paul,' she said, 'you never saw me learning a new and foully difficult piece of music, did you?'

'That's true.'

'I would work at it for hours, slowly, minutely and repetitively, without appearing to make any headway at first, until eventually it began to take shape. I met lots of challenges on the way but never at any stage was I frustrated.'

'So it's a challenge.'

'It's certainly that, but it has its rewards.' Her expression softened and she tapped his forearm gently. 'Does it really worry you, Paul?'

'Not now.'

'But it did.'

He smiled self-consciously. 'Call it neighbourly concern.'

'I appreciate your concern.'

'So,' he asked, changing the subject, 'what diversions have you got lined up for the rest of the day?'

'I'm taking Nicola for a haircut at two o'clock.'

'My granddad used to do the same with me when I was a youngster. I didn't appreciate it at the time.'

'This is different, Paul. Do you remember her looking at that photo of Aunt Ellen and saying how much she'd like to have her hair done like hers? She's going to have a classic bob, and my guess is it will make a huge difference to her self-confidence.'

'In that case it has to be a good idea.'

'And then we'll go to Harrison's for tea. It's extravagant of me, I know, but I don't have my granddaughter to stay every holiday.'

'You will if you keep taking her to Harrison's.'

'It's not the teatime treats that attract her but they're nevertheless there to be enjoyed.' She decided to share the indulgence. 'Would you like to join us?'

Paul blinked at the unexpected invitation. 'Thank you, I'd like that very much.' He added, 'Will I be allowed boiled eggs and toast soldiers too?'

'Only if you're very good and keep coming up with ideas.'

The prospect seemed to stimulate an immediate response, because he said, 'I know what you could do.'

'Vis-à-vis what?'

'The particulars of Mrs Whatsit's demise.'

'Go on.'

'The death of a prominent member of the community would attract the attention of the press. The local rag might even have sent a reporter to the funeral.'

'*The Cullington Herald*?' Plum didn't take the local paper and remembered its name with difficulty.

'That's what they call it now, but it was *The Cullington Evening Intelligencer* before the war.'

'What a glorious name. Do you think they'll have back numbers from so long ago?'

'The *Herald* won't. There's barely room in the office for the people who work there. No, you'll find the back copies on microfilm at the public library.'

* * *

'Can I help you?' With an effort, the girl on the reception desk at the salon transferred her attention from her mobile phone.

'I have a date with two of your patrons and they said they'd be ready about now. That's Mrs Harvey and her granddaughter.'

The girl looked dazed and then realisation dawned. 'Oh, you mean Plum and Nicola.'

'And I thought this was a high-class establishment.'

The girl was unabashed. 'I don't think they'll be long. Would you like to take a seat?'

He was about to accept the offer when he heard Plum's voice nearby. 'Don't let him sit down. He'll fall asleep.'

Paul remained standing and held out his hands to greet Nicola, at the same time appraising her newly-cut bob with a photographer's professional eye. 'Nicola,' he said, 'without a word of exaggeration, you look lovely.'

'Thank you.' She smiled self-consciously because the compliment was clearly genuine. It was also a new experience for her.

'And so do you, Plum.' He stepped back theatrically to admire her coif as she settled the bill and made a new appointment.

'Thank you, Paul.' She smiled. 'Now I know it's all been worthwhile.'

Half-smiling, the receptionist looked from one to the other, possibly wondering about their relationship. It was a mystery that would tease her for a while longer because, leaving no further clues, they took their leave of her and left the salon.

In the four months since Plum's return she'd come to accept the absence or relocation of several of Cullington's landmarks and could be forgiven for asking, 'Is the public library still beside the station?'

'It certainly is,' confirmed Paul.

'Splendid.' It was reassuring that another building of treasured memory had survived in her absence and she made a mental inventory of those she'd noticed so far. It included the Railway Station, Harrison's Coffee House, the Town Hall, the Wool Exchange, and now the Public Library.

'The interior has changed quite a lot,' said Paul as they walked. 'They've modernised it as far as possible, but it's a listed building and there are limits to what they can do.'

'Quite right,' said Plum. 'We can't stop the rush of progress altogether but we must make a token show of resistance.'

'Some of that progress can be very useful,' Paul reminded her. 'You'll use a microfilm reader this afternoon, and possibly look at records from *The Times* on a database.'

'It's a prosaic language, isn't it?' She considered that briefly, thankful that Paul would be there to translate as well as supervise. She asked, 'How do you know about this kind of thing?'

'I've used the reference library sometimes to find old pictures, and computers came into the trade some years ago. I suppose you either fight shy of something like that or you take advantage of it.'

'I've always found pianos reassuringly mechanical.'

Nicola, who had been following the conversation, said, 'There's a digital piano at school.'

'I suspected there might be,' said Plum. 'Does it play itself or did it come with a robot to do that?'

'It can play by itself. It has recorded music and you can record your own on it.'

Plum nodded grudgingly. 'I can see that being quite useful for self-appraisal.'

'What's that?'

'Listening to yourself to find ways of improving your performance.'

Nicola was inclined to be dismissive. 'Mrs Holroyd just records songs on it so that Mrs Dyson or Miss Thompson can take choir practice when she's not there.'

'That sounds like a fair pooling of skills,' said Plum. 'I'm learning lots of new things this afternoon.'

'And you're going to learn more,' said Paul as they mounted the steps of the Victorian building.

The reference library was off the lobby, and they waited until a librarian came to them. Paul explained that they wanted to find an obituary from 1922 in *The Times* and to look through numbers of *The Cullington Evening Intelligencer* from the same year.

'You're lucky,' the librarian told him, 'because we only have the *Intelligencer* from nineteen-twenty onwards. Have you used a microfilm reader before?'

'Yes, and I've searched *The Times*.'

'Right, I'll get you the microfilm for nineteen-twenty-two and then you can decide which you want to do first.'

Paul decided to start with *The Times*, and Plum watched with the fascination of the technically innocent.

'Now,' he said, keying in the parameters, 'we're looking for an obituary or death notice in March 'twenty-two and the name is Bainbridge. Have you got a Christian name?'

'Yes, it's Elizabeth. That's the only one I know.'

'Here's a notice,' he said. 'There doesn't seem to be an obituary.'

Plum sat beside him to read the record.

Mrs Elizabeth Mary Bainbridge née Vaughan, widow of the late Alfred Ernest Bainbridge and mother of the late Edward Albert and of Ellen Bainbridge of Cullington, Yorkshire, died on 4th March. Funeral to be held at All Saints' Church, Cullington on 17th March at 10.00 a.m.

'At least it tells us the date of the funeral,' she said, trying to disguise her disappointment.

'Yes.' Paul closed the database and picked up the reel of microfilm. 'We
have the choice of two readers,' he said. 'I think we'll use the new, space-age one with the electric winder.'

'I'm sure it's the obvious choice,' said Plum. Completely baffled, she watched him thread the film on to the machine and adjust the focus. 'In my ignorance,' she said, 'I expected microfilm to be weenie and fit into a tiny camera like the ones spies use in the old films I pretend not to watch. This is just like thirty-five millimetre film without holes.'

'Those tiny cameras were eight-millimetre sub-miniature, and this really is thirty-five millimetre film without sprocket holes,' he confirmed. 'Now, Nicola, I'm putting you in charge of the winder. To go down the page and on to the next page you turn this knob to the right. To fast-forward it you turn it and hold it. Okay?'

'Right.' Nicola put her hand on the knob and stared at the screen with stern concentration.

'Now, we're on Monday the 2nd of January, so the 4th of March is some way off, but let's look through a few pages first, just for practice.'

Not surprisingly there was very little real news, and most of the comment was about the record low rainfall of 1921, and the New Year Honours Lists, which were evidently big news even in Cullington. Plum spotted the name of the composer Ethel Smyth and learned that she had been made a Dame of the British Empire. This prompted questions from Nicola, who was surprised to learn that female composers were rare in those times.

After a few more pages Paul looked at his watch. 'I think we should move on, Nicola,' he said.

His conscientious research assistant twisted the knob to the right and held it there whilst several months of 1922 flew through the reader at an alarming speed. When she released her grip she found herself looking at Wednesday, the 5th of April.

'Don't worry,' Paul told her. 'Just turn the knob to the left and go back.' The reader reversed slowly through early April and most of March until it reached Monday the 6th.

'Okay, let's go forward. I doubt if there'll be anything in this one but we'll check anyway.' They found Births, Marriages and Deaths, which confirmed Paul's doubts, and moved on. In the same column on the 7th they found the same notice as the one they'd read in The Times.

'It's becoming rather predictable,' said Plum, conscious that she was wasting the others' time.

'Not at all. We're not finished yet.' Paul was issuing instructions to Nicola, who was now more in control of the winder. They examined several issues without finding an obituary, so they pressed on until they came to Saturday the 18th. Nicola was the first to see it. 'Look,' she cried, earning a glare from another reader close by. 'There it is.' She pointed at the screen excitedly.

'Good girl,' said Plum, 'but try to keep your voice down.' They read the report together.

The funeral of Mrs Elizabeth Bainbridge was held at All Saints' Church, Cullington yesterday at ten a.m. The Reverend Canon Matthew Peacock presided.

It gave details of family members attending and went on to describe the service. There was a list of the readings and hymns, which suggested to Plum and Paul that funerals must have been generally lengthier in those days. More importantly there was an outline of the eulogy. One sentence in particular caught their attention.

She spent many a pleasant hour reading in her favourite armchair, where her maid, who was about to serve lunch, found her, having spoken with her only half-an-hour earlier.

'So much for dying in neglect,' said Plum triumphantly. 'She died within half-an-hour of being apparently fit and well.'

'Just as you suspected,' said Paul.

'Yes, and now we can go to Harrison's for tea because you've both earned it.'

28

'The organ is a strange instrument,' said Hugh. 'The only gradual things about it are the enclosed pipes in the swell. They can be made to crescendo and decrescendo, but that's all. Everything else happens in defined stages and you get either very little change or a complete surprise.' The last of the post-funeral gathering had left and Hugh was free to express his feelings about the music he'd heard that morning.

'The organ at All Saints is a poor example, in any case,' said Ellen, 'although they should soon be able to have it repaired properly. That's when they receive Mother's bequest.'

'Really?' Hugh had no idea Mrs Bainbridge was musically inclined.

'Oh yes, she'd been helping out with the cost of running repairs for some time.'

'Was she keen on organ music?' It still seemed odd.

'No, but she supported the church. The organ was just one of its liabilities.'

'Well, I'm glad she did, because anything that can improve the sound of that thing is worth the outlay. I thought it was going to die on us this morning.'

She smiled wryly. 'That might have created a merciful diversion.' Ellen was still feeling bruised by veiled remarks that had been made about the timing and secrecy of the wedding.

'Far be it from me to criticise your family—'

'Nevertheless, feel free.'

'Well, I appreciate the fact that no one is supposed to look happy at a funeral, but most of them gave me the impression they'd be a joyless crowd at any gathering, about as dour as my family on a good day, and most of them bear the essence of gloom.'

Suddenly she was laughing. 'They sound awful.'

'Wait 'til you meet them. There's Uncle Horace and Aunt Maria. Her name, incidentally, really does rhyme with "higher", not "here". I mention it because to mispronounce it is to cause grave offence.'

'She sounds like fun.'

'Believe me when I tell you that those two are the harbingers of disaster. They've got the Ides of March and the whole blessed calendar marked out for gloom, doom and catastrophe.'

'Oh dear.' She smiled at his description. 'Did you invent those two to cheer me up?'

'I couldn't invent two people as awful as them, and they're not alone; there's their son Cyril, who says little but gives the impression that the utterances of others are faintly ridiculous. He goes about with a permanent sneer on his upper lip. I once advised him to grow a moustache to cover it, but he treated that as a frivolous suggestion.' He waved aside the unpleasant image of Cyril. 'Worst of all,' he said, 'is Cyril's brother Sidney.' Then he hesitated.

'Please describe him. I need the diversion.'

'He's ... let me think. No, he's too awful to describe. Just pray you never meet him.'

'All right, I shall.' But she was smiling. 'I don't believe a word of it,' she said.

'That's your privilege.'

'And I have so many of them now. Shall we have tea?'

'I think so.'

Ellen rang the bell, and very shortly Hannah came. 'Yes, ma'am?'

'We'd like tea, please, Hannah.'

'Very good, ma'am.'

As the door closed, Ellen said, 'I think I preferred "Miss Ellen". "Ma'am" is too close to "mama".'

'That's true.'

The notion seemed to give rise to consideration, because she said, 'We should discuss the names.'

'Whose names?'

'Our firstborn's names, of course.'

'Of course.'

'I don't know how much thought you've given this subject, but if we have a boy I'd rather like one of his names to be Edward, after my brother. How do you feel about that?'

In truth Hugh had given the matter little thought, September being some time away. 'I'm more than happy with that,' he said.

'Have you any ideas?'

'Well,' he said, 'I wonder about calling him Albert, after Bertie.'

'That's just what I was going to suggest.'

'Edward Albert,' he mused.

'Or Albert Edward, like one of the Princes.'

'There's no law against it.' He closed his eyes in thought and said, 'Either way we'll need to decide on different names if it's a girl.'

'It would be advisable. What were your mother's names?'

'Beatrice and Victoria.'

'My mother's names were Elizabeth and Mary, and I'm not desperately keen on either of them. How do you feel about yours?'

Hugh tried to visualise a tiny baby called Beatrice Victoria or Victoria Beatrice. Eventually, he said, 'I think "Beatrice" sounds old-fashioned. It belongs to the last century, and I'm afraid "Victoria" is equally dated but I like it for all that. Maybe we could give her three names and Victoria could be one of them, just to give her room for choice in later life.'

At that point, Hannah interrupted their deliberations by arriving with the tea.

'Thank you, Hannah.'

'Very good, ma'am.'

They resumed their task and eventually agreed on three names for their unborn daughter. She would be called Jane Louise Victoria, and for the sake of fairness they decided on a third boy's name. Their son would be called Albert Edward George. A day of solemnity, tension and suspicion had ended in consensus.

29

As Nicola's holiday drew toward its close, Plum attempted to take stock of all her granddaughter had achieved during that time. The multiplication tables were possibly the least of her accomplishments but that didn't worry Plum at all, because the child's progress in reading dramatically outweighed any shortcomings in numeracy, and she felt sure that spelling and punctuation would follow in time. By far the success that gave Plum the greatest satisfaction was Nicola's improved self-image, although she knew that Paul deserved some of the credit for that.

They were currently working together on some photographs so that she would have something to take home. Paul had said it was going to be a portfolio to be proud of, and Plum trusted him.

She heard the kitchen door being opened and closed, and then Paul came in. 'Nicola's putting the coffee on,' he reported.

'I don't know what I'll do without her.'

'Life will certainly be different.' He took his usual seat and said, 'We've been listening to *Rhapsody in Blue* and Nicola's confused. I said she'd better ask you about it.'

'I don't understand the name,' said Nicola, coming in from the kitchen.

Plum wasn't at all surprised. 'A rhapsody,' she said, 'is a piece of music that communicates an emotion. It may be about a country or a place that the composer loves so much he has to write a piece of music about it. Gershwin was obviously thinking about America, because Blues is a kind of American popular music.'

Nicola was still struggling. 'What's Blues about, then?'

'It's black American music that stems originally from black suffering, anger, pleasure and a whole range of emotions. It's not always about sadness, even though people talk about feeling "blue" when they're sad.'

'But why do they call it Blues?'

'It's possibly because it uses "blue" notes. Come over here and I'll show you.' She sat at the piano and lifted the fall. 'A normal scale sounds like this.' She played the scale of C. 'A great many songs take their notes from it, but sometimes Blues singers and musicians flatten some of the notes to suggest the emotion they want to communicate, like this.' She improvised briefly on 'Three Blind Mice,' inserting E flat, G flat and B flat to give it a Blues effect. 'These are called "blue notes",' she explained.

Clearly frustrated, Nicola said, 'But they're not blue. That one,' and she pointed to E flat is orangey-yellow, and this one is purple.' She pointed to G flat.

Plum stared at her momentarily and then asked, 'Does every note have a colour?'

'Yes.' Impatience gave way to frustration. 'I said that at school and they laughed at me. They said I was mental.'

'Oh, but you're not.' Plum held out her arm and Nicola joined her on the stool. 'And I'm not laughing at you. Tell me, do you see colours with all sounds, not just music?'

'Yes, but they're not as nice as the music colours.'

'And do you see colours when you taste something?'

'No.'

'Can you taste music?'

Nicola snorted. 'Don't be silly.'

'Some people can.'

As Nicola began to look a little more reassured, Paul continued to stare at Plum uncomprehendingly.

'Trust me, Paul. Nicola has a special gift.'

'Does that mean I haven't got something wrong with me?' For the first time during their conversation Nicola was beginning to look happy.

'There's absolutely nothing wrong with you; in fact you have something others might envy. You have senses – mainly hearing and sight – that communicate with each other. It means you can enjoy some of the best things in life more fully than most people. It's a wonderful thing, Nicola, and you must never think there's anything wrong with you.'

'They wouldn't stop laughing at school.'

'Who wouldn't, the other children or the teachers?'

Nicola shook her head. 'I daren't tell the teachers. I thought they'd tell me I was daft as well.' She ran her finger over the white keys and said, 'I've always liked the colours of the piano. I sometimes play around with our piano at home, just mixing colours.'

'Would you like to learn the piano?'

She looked down at the keyboard unsurely. 'Yes, but I always thought it would be too hard.'

'You thought multiplication and reading were hard. Just think what you can do now.' She made a decision. 'Paul, will you help yourself to coffee? Nicola, get whatever you want from the fridge while I make a phone call.' She slid off the piano stool and dialled Heather's number. She hoped Heather would be at home, because she was more likely to have a sensible conversation with her than with Nigel.

'Hello?'

'Heather, thank goodness for that. It's Plum.'

'What's the matter, Plum?'

'Absolutely nothing's the matter. Listen, Heather, when Nicola goes back to school you must have her tested by a psychologist or someone of that ilk, because I'm convinced she has synaesthesia. It just needs to be diagnosed. If it comes to that, I suppose one of your people could do it.'

'What? I mean how do you know this?'

'She sees bursts of colour whenever she hears sounds. I'm not sure at this stage what other senses are affected but that'll surely come out in a test.'

'Good heavens. You know, I remember her telling me she didn't like Mondays, and I thought at first it was because of going back to school, but she told me Mondays were yellow and grey and she wasn't keen on those colours. Apparently Wednesday has the best colour. I'm afraid I dismissed the conversation at the time as childish nonsense.'

'You weren't the only one, Heather. Nicola's been living in her own multi-coloured world, afraid to talk about it in case she's held to ridicule, as she once was at school.'

'Not by a teacher, I hope?'

'No, we've been through that. She's never told any of the staff.'

Heather was silent for a moment, and then she said, 'It could easily have some bearing on her numeracy problem as well. I just hadn't considered it before.'

'It wasn't obvious.'

'I believe it's hereditary, although it's not bound to affect every generation. I certainly can't think of anyone in my family who's been affected by it.'

'It may have come down the Linthwaite line or possibly my mother's side. Like you, I haven't been aware of it but it's a possibility.'

'Well, I'll get on to that straight away, Plum. Thank you for telling me.'

'It's no trouble. Oh, there's one more thing.'

'What's that?'

'Nicola would like to learn the piano. I'm more than happy to teach her if you have no objection.'

'None at all. I used to play when I was younger, and it'll be nice for Nicola to learn.'

'I'll need to see her every week.'

'I'm sure we can arrange that. Thank you, Plum.'

When Plum came off the phone she said, 'Well, I'm sure you managed to follow that conversation, Nicola. You're going to have piano lessons with me.'

'Every week?'

'Every single week.'

'Great!' They had a spontaneous hug while Paul looked on, baffled.

'I'll tell you about synaesthesia later,' Plum promised him.

30

May

Hugh arrived at number one-hundred-and-fifty in good time to meet the man in charge of the household removal, and was surprised to find Ellen with wet cheeks.

'What on earth's the matter, darling?'

She attempted a smile of greeting. 'I've just given Mrs Whittaker and Hannah their final wages. They've gone now.'

'They'd been with you a long time, hadn't they?' He held out his arms in consolation.

'Since before I was born,' she confirmed, laying her head against his chest. 'They were part of my childhood.'

'But it was what they wanted. You said so.'

'Yes, it's just hard to part.' She was momentarily silent and then she said, 'It's awful that I feel more sadness at losing them than I did about my mother.'

'But you said they showed you more affection than she did when you were a child.'

'That's true.' She broke away from him to blow her nose. 'Oh well,' she said, 'life goes on. Thank goodness Mrs Naylor agreed to have her hours increased.'

'She's glad of it. She's a widow, you know.'

'I didn't know that. How did you find her?'

'She found me, as it happened. Her late husband was in my platoon in the early days, and she thought I might know of someone who needed domestic help.'

'And you did.'

'Yes, I was the one who needed help, and a first-class help she's been.'

As they sat down together he said, 'Do you remember on the day of your mother's funeral you asked me to describe my cousin Sidney?'

'The indescribable one?'

'Yes, that's the one. He's announced that he'll call on me tomorrow. I've agreed to meet him at T' Doctor's 'Ouse.' He spoke the name in the local accent.

'Where?'

'Our marital home. The locals still refer to it as "T' Doctor's 'Ouse" because it was my father's for so many years. In a community like this, even the humblest of traditions assume a kind of permanence. At all events, you have the choice between meeting my egregious cousin and avoiding him completely. I'll be happy to find you a good excuse.'

She laughed. 'I can't believe he's so awful. What does he want?'

'I don't know, but you're quite right to suspect that he wants something. He wouldn't be Sidney if he weren't seeking favours or foraging for something, although it beats me why, when he made a small fortune out of the war.'

'How did he do that?'

'His family manufacture leather goods. You can imagine the demand for belts, holsters, tack and so on in wartime.'

'So he never served in the war.'

'No, he was unfit for service. It was a good thing, really. He'd have been disastrous for morale.'

* * *

Hugh had just seen an enormous wardrobe, once the property of Mrs Bainbridge, being carried upstairs, and he was wondering about the sheer strength of the men doing the carrying, when Mrs Naylor came to him and said, 'Mr Sidney Linthwaite is here, sir. He says you are expecting him.'

'Thank you, Mrs Naylor. Will you show him into the study and then bring coffee for three of us?'

'Very good, sir.'

He found Ellen on the first landing. In a tone laced with doom, he said, 'You wanted to meet Sidney. He's in the study.'

'Oh, now I'll see if you were exaggerating or just making it up.' She added, 'I only want to meet him. I shan't stay for long.'

'No one ever does.' They went down to the study and Hugh opened the door.

'Good morning, Sidney. I trust I find you well.' His cousin was examining the piano as if he might be thinking of buying it.

'Well enough, Hugh. And you?'

'Very well, thank you.' Turning to Ellen, he said, 'Darling, this is my cousin Sidney. Sidney, my wife Ellen.'

'Ellen, I'm delighted to meet you. And please accept my sympathy on your bereavement.'

'Thank you.' She accepted Sidney's limp hand. Had he taken the trouble, Hugh would have described him as a limp man. He seemed unable to stand up straight, but stood hunched and leaning a little to one side. His features were bland and his eyes lacked depth, although they appeared to scrutinize Ellen in some detail.

'You received my letter, of course,' said Sidney, 'but I must offer you both my good wishes in person.'

'Thank you.' Hugh waited for Ellen to take her seat before waving Sidney to a chair.

'Your wedding was, let's say, unexpected.'

'We were expecting it,' Hugh told him, 'and that's what really matters. We also got the simple ceremony we preferred.'

'Oh, that's your affair, of course.' Sidney waved a limp hand. 'But now, presumably, you're moving two homes into one?'

'Yes, we are,' said Ellen, 'and because of that I have to ask you to excuse me. I must be on hand to advise the men. I'm glad to have met you.'

'And I, Ellen. Hopefully, we shall meet again before long.'

'Who knows?' Ellen opened the door. 'Goodbye, then.' She left the room, leaving Hugh with the predictable impression that she had found his cousin less than beguiling.

'So,' said Sidney, 'I imagine it won't be long before you leave teaching to those unfortunates who have to labour for their crust.'

'I left the school at the end of last term. We're lucky enough to have an excellent booking agent.'

'And the rest, eh?' The half-smile was meaningful.

'I have a small income, it's true. But tell me about yourself. I trust business is as brisk as ever.' Hugh had little interest in the fortunes of Sidney's side of the family but he was keen to shift the attention away from his own affairs.

'Business is good,' said Sidney, 'and could improve even more with the right investment.' Before he could say more, the door opened and Mrs Naylor came into the study carrying a tray laden with coffee, cups and saucers, cream and sugar.

'You can leave it on the desk, Mrs Naylor. I'll pour it,' said Hugh, removing an opened letter from the blotter. 'I'm afraid Mrs Linthwaite had to leave us to supervise the removal.'

'That's all right, sir. I'll make some more coffee for her.'

'Thank you, Mrs Naylor. That's very thoughtful of you.'

'It's no trouble, sir.'

Sidney watched her leave the study and asked, 'How many servants have you now?'

'Only Mrs Naylor. She was my housekeeper before we asked her to stay on as cook-general.'

'Really?' Sidney seemed mildly surprised.

'One is all we need in a house of this size,' said Hugh. 'But you were telling me about your business, something about investment.' He poured coffee into two cups, determined to keep the conversation from straying.

'Yes, so that we can expand we need to invest in machinery and labour so that in these straitened times we can take a greater share of existing markets.'

'I can see that, but what's stopping you?'

Sidney accepted his coffee, added a lump of sugar and stirred it before replying. 'It's a matter of liquid capital,' he said.

Hugh's suspicion had been correct. Now that he knew the reason for his cousin's visit any suggestion of sympathy he might have felt evaporated in an instant, although his voice was level when he asked, 'What happened to the fortune you made out of the war? Don't tell me a million men died in vain.'

Sidney ignored the jibe. 'Hugh,' he said, 'you're a schoolmaster. It's not your fault that you know nothing of business. Liquidity and profit, you see, are distinct entities. A business can be highly profitable, as ours certainly is, but at the same time it can be temporarily in need of cash investment.'

'I see.' Sidney had prepared his request with characteristic lack of subtlety, but Hugh was nevertheless surprised by the directness that followed.

'I'm offering you a chance to invest in a profitable and growing enterprise. It's an opportunity you'd be foolish to turn down, because I see great times ahead.'

'Why should that appeal to a schoolmaster who knows nothing about business?'

Sidney smiled faintly. 'I wondered when you'd throw that one back at me. Look, Hugh, you needn't concern yourself with the running of the business. You'd be a sort of sleeping partner.'

It sounded depressingly familiar to Hugh. 'I imagine you mean a partner who's sleepy enough to disregard caution altogether and lend you money.'

'My dear chap, you really must think of it as an investment.'

'Oh, I could think of it as all manner of things.'

'Well, I suppose that's a start.'

'As I see it, the only difficulty is that I have no money to lend or invest.'

Sidney looked at him as he might regard a dull-witted office boy. 'I was under the impression,' he said, 'that you'd recently married a major shareholder in Adams and Bainbridge and that you had just sold a particularly substantial property.'

'Oh yes, I can't deny any of that.'

'In that case, what is the problem?' Sidney's gentle entreaty was giving way to impatience.

'The problem is that it's Ellen's money, not mine. I haven't a brass farthing beyond my earnings and a very modest annuity.'

'You could persuade her to make the investment. She'd surely agree to it.'

Hugh struggled to control his twitch. 'How can you know that when you've only just met her, and even then very briefly?'

'But surely you're in charge of her affairs.'

'Absolutely not. Why should she trust a schoolmaster who knows nothing about business?'

'Damn it, Hugh.' Impatience had now become exasperation. 'It wouldn't mean a thing to her. She wouldn't even notice it. She's a woman, for goodness' sake.'

Hugh rose to his feet, his patience now expended. 'Sidney,' he said, 'come with me. We'll pick up your hat and coat on the way out.'

'Why? Where are we going?'

'We are going to the door, and then you may go wherever your fancy takes you.' He bundled him through the doorway and along the passage to the front door, which he opened for his cousin's exit. 'You're no longer welcome in this house. I never want to see you nor hear from you again.'

Sidney took his coat and hat from the stand, his features flushed with outrage. As he stepped over the threshold he turned to say, 'You're making a grave mistake. I shan't forget this.'

'The only mistake I made was in agreeing to see you. Now, go before I help you on your way.'

Having closed the door, he found Ellen beside him.

'What on earth was that about?'

'Don't worry about it, darling. He was only being his obnoxious self.'

'I must say I didn't find him at all appealing. What did he want?'

'It's not important,' he said. 'He wanted me to invest in his company but, being Sidney, he put it to me as his right and due, and when I told him I had no money he became presumptuous and arrogant so I showed him to the door.'

'What an unpleasant surprise it must have been.'

'It was no surprise. I've known him a long time.'

After a moment's consideration she said, 'You know, if you did hear of an investment that really interested you, I could always help.'

'I know you could, and I'm grateful, but I'll have nothing to do with Sidney.'

'All right, we'll leave it there.'

'Yes, we have more important things to consider.' The immediate concern was the removal, then the need to practise for their next two engagements, which would be Ellen's last for some time. They had to consider her condition. Her pregnancy wasn't yet obvious but it soon would be.

31

'Synaesthesia,' said Plum, 'is the reaction to a stimulus by two or more of the senses.'

Paul looked anxiously at a large, black cloud that was drawing ever closer. 'I think we'd better decamp,' he said. 'Your place or mine?' They were already in his garden, so he made the decision. 'Mine, I think. I've made some biscuits.'

'You're very bad for my diet, Paul.' Nevertheless, she followed him into his kitchen, where Paul switched the kettle on and they sat at the table.

'So this thing Nicola's got is a bit like crossed telephone lines?'

'I suppose so. Some people can taste and feel sounds as well as hearing them.'

'That is amazing. But you don't see it as a disability?'

'No, I don't. If anything, it's a special facility; in fact most synaesthetes say they wouldn't choose to be at all different. There are some drawbacks, I suppose. Some, although not all, have a numeracy problem; with others it's their sense of direction, but generally it's a gift rather than a disability.' She opened her bag and took out a strip of tablets.

'Is it your arm?' Paul filled a glass with water and put it on the table for her.

'Yes, it can be "a right bugger".' She smiled thinly. 'That's how Tyler the postman describes his back complaint.' She pushed two of the tablets out of their foil packaging and swallowed them. 'I try not to take these things too often,' she said. 'Apart from the risk of addiction, they apparently lose their effectiveness after a while.' She put the glass down again and said bleakly, 'I suspect they already have.' She watched Paul get up to brew the tea and put biscuits on a plate, and said, 'We were talking about synaesthesia, weren't we?'

'Yes, but it's not desperately important.'

'It beats talking about chronic disability and pain-killers that don't work.'

'Agreed.' He put a plate of home-made ginger biscuits and chocolate-chip cookies on the table.

'Nicola's problem with arithmetic is partly to do with logic as well.'

'Oh?'

'Yes, if she thinks long enough about it, she knows that nine and seven make sixteen, but if nine is a green number and seven is yellow they also add up to fourteen, which is rather like the earth wire when you're wiring a plug, apparently. It's been years since I wired a plug, and I couldn't even begin to do it now.' Using her right hand, she lifted her left arm gingerly and rested it on the table.

'I could find you a sling if you think it might help.'

'Could you?'

'One moment.' He slipped out to the dark room and returned with a foam plastic sling.

'Your dark room is full of surprises,' she said as he looped it over her head, 'and so are you. Thank you.'

'When I employed staff I had to be tooled up and trained in first-aid.' He stood back to view the finished job and nodded his satisfaction. 'Shall we sit comfortably in the sitting room?' He seemed to take her agreement for granted, because he took out a tray and put the teapot and everything else on it.

'You spoil me, Paul.' She stood up and followed him.

'Sit wherever you're going to be most comfortable,' he advised.

She nodded and took the sofa while he poured the tea. 'I've got an appointment with my doctor tomorrow,' she told him.

'Well done. Getting one with mine is a feat of timing and dogged persistence.' He put her tea down on the low table in front of the sofa. 'You must have qualities I haven't yet noticed.'

She smiled. 'You're hedging in case it's embarrassing, aren't you?'

'Of course. Doctors and women are a cringe-making combination.'

'It's nothing like that. I'm going to ask him to refer me to an orthopaedic surgeon so that I can be rid of this thing permanently.'

He was silent for a few seconds, and then asked, 'Do you mean amputation?'

'Yes, it's a source of frequent and severe pain and it's of absolutely no use to me.' She studied his expression and for once found it impossible to read, so she asked, 'How will you see me with only one arm?'

'I think the fact that you're asking me that suggests you're not completely decided.'

'I am really.'

'In that case I imagine I'll see you just as I do now but I'll be very relieved that you're free of pain.'

That made her smile. 'You're in good company, Paul. I asked Nicola the same question before she went home.'

'What did she say?'

'She said she would love me every bit as much as she does now and be very happy because I'd no longer be in pain.'

He nodded, smiling. 'Two minds in complete agreement. What did Nigel say?'

'Oh, let me think. He said it was an irrevocable step – if that's not stating the obvious I don't know what is – and he asked me if I'd thought it through, and then told me it was a decision only I could make.' She laughed shortly. 'Heather was more human about it. She used a lot of socio-psychological mumbo-jumbo, but basically said she was right behind me, which was unexpectedly comforting.'

'I'm glad about that, because I've been wondering whether to offer you a biscuit or a couple of boiled eggs with toast sailors, just to cheer you up.'

'Just talking with you cheers me up no end.' She performed a deliberate double-take and asked, 'Why toast sailors?'

'When you cut buttered toast and hold up a piece to dunk in your egg it looks drunken and disreputable, not stiff and smart like a soldier.'

'I don't think I've never looked at soldiers or sailors in such detail.' She smiled at his kindness and said, 'You know, you mustn't worry about me. I'm quite resilient. I've had to be after some of the knocks I've taken.'

'I imagine you have. You were going to tell me about one of them.' He added, 'Of course, you mustn't feel you have to. It was just something we were talking about earlier.'

'Oh?'

'The second-worst time of your life,' he prompted.

Then she remembered. 'You mean the time I became pregnant and had to get married.'

'Had to?'

'There was no alternative. I was a student and I had no money. He was teaching by that time, so he had a kind of income.'

'What was his name?'

'Oh, I'm sorry. This was Stephen Walsh, known to all his women as "Stevie". He could charm the knickers off a nun and was completely self-centred. I was twenty-one and I still had a year to do at college when I met him.' She looked down into her teacup, wondering why she still resented him so many years on. 'When I broke the news at home, my mother reacted much as you'd expect a northern middle-class mother to react until she settled for wringing her hands for what seemed like days on end, thankful that my father wasn't around to share the disgrace.'

'So there was no support from home.'

'None whatsoever, although most of the condemnation came from a different quarter. Do you remember my telling you about my cousin Malcolm?'

'The one you met in Harrison's?'

'That's right. Well, if you'd seen the way his father behaved you'd have thought I'd embarked on a career in prostitution. My aunt took a softer line but I think she was under Uncle Joseph's thumb, so there wasn't a lot she could do. She did give me twenty pounds, though, when I went back to London.'

'What about Malcolm?'

She had to think about that. 'I really don't know that he was ever told. He was heavily involved with his studies at the time. At all events, he's never been less than courteous to me.' She thought again. 'Malcolm is infinitely more like his mother than his father.'

'All the same, what a horrible time it must have been.'

'I spent most of that Easter holiday in tears. There was one day, though, when I visited Uncle Hugh, and he was so kind that I came close to telling him about my problem. Naturally I didn't. I was afraid he would think less of me.'

'Have a biscuit.' He offered her the plate.

'It's all right, Paul.' She smiled. 'I'm not going to cry.'

'Have a biscuit anyway.'

'Thank you.' She took one of his chocolate-chip cookies. 'I left the College that summer,' she said. 'I had to because the baby was due in October. We had a flat in Battersea, distant enough from Chelsea to be affordable and also handy for day-school pupils. After Nigel was born, I taught and practised with him beside me in his cot and later in his playpen.'

Paul merely nodded as he usually did when she was telling him a story. He was a rewarding listener.

'Steve chose the worst time to misbehave. Nigel was teething, sleep was a forgotten luxury, I was working under impossible conditions, and now my husband told me he had a girlfriend and she also had a problem.' She accepted another cup of tea and went on. 'He cleared off and the divorce duly came through. It was at his expense and he was ordered to pay maintenance as well. Even so, it was hard to find any sympathy for him.'

'I can't imagine how you coped with all that.'

'I just had to, I suppose.'

'But how did you move on from that to the career you eventually had?'

'It was a combination of hard work, good luck and meeting the right people. When Nigel was three I took him to a play group twice a week because it was all I could afford and it allowed me to practise without interruption. That was where, by sheer good fortune, I met someone whose sister worked for Friedlander and Stein the booking agents, and she got me an introduction. After that, work began to come in, slowly at first and then more frequently, and during a visit to the agents' office I met my second husband Tom.'

'You must have felt like Cinderella.'

'Just a bit,' she laughed. 'When they found me my first recital I had to buy a second-hand evening dress from a charity shop. They were right out of glass slippers.'

Paul couldn't help smiling. 'So that's the story behind all these CDs,' he said, pointing to the bookshelf behind him.

'Yes.' She levered herself off the sofa and stood up to examine them. 'Good heavens, Paul,' she said after a quick look, 'you must have almost everything I ever recorded.'

'Almost,' he agreed. 'There are some LPs on the top shelf.'

'I don't believe this.' She reached up and pulled one out. It was a record of the Paganini Studies of Franz Liszt and there was a photograph of her on the sleeve. 'Oh,' she said, 'I don't look like that now.'

'No, you've improved with age.'

'Paul, you old flatterer, don't stop there.' She replaced the LP on the shelf and remembered something else. 'I was going to let you have that remastered recording of Uncle Hugh's, wasn't I? Was it Cesar Franck's Symphonic Variations?'

'That's right.'

'I'll bring it over.' She sat down again. 'You know,' she said, 'I must look through the rest of that pile of Uncle Hugh's things. I've been rather distracted lately.'

32

September 1922

Hugh imagined he must have been in the waiting room about an hour. There was no clock and, as he never wore nor carried a watch, he could only guess at the time. He was more than usually conscious of it because, for almost every second since Ellen's labour pains had begun, he had endured the worst anxiety he had ever known. Even at the height of battle he'd never felt helpless; he'd been too occupied for that, and he'd even been able to adopt a patchy kind of fatalism under shellfire. Many succumbed to shellshock and neurosis at such times but his horrors came much later and even then they occurred in relatively short spells. By comparison, waiting in that room was undiluted torture because there was nothing he could do.

He remembered his relief when the doctor arrived at the house a little after midnight, and the reassuring feeling that Ellen was in safe hands. That was until the same doctor came out of the bedroom to call an ambulance. Ellen was being passed to another pair of safe hands, which were clearly now finding the task far from straightforward. He tried to swallow. His mouth was dry and his tongue felt like an unwanted visitor.

The sound of brisk, business-like footsteps came from the corridor, criss-crossing and occasionally, from the fragments of conversation he overheard, converging and parting as some new task made its demands.

After some time a nurse opened the door to ask if he would like a cup of tea. Hugh stood up immediately and asked, 'What's happening? My wife's been in there for more than an hour.'

The nurse opened her mouth to speak and then hesitated before saying, 'It's not a straightforward birth, Mr Linthwaite. It's going to take time.'

'I already know that. What's the problem?'

'There's a complication.'

'Yes, I know that. What kind of complication are you talking about?'

Once again the nurse hesitated before speaking. 'There's nothing to worry about,' she said. 'Now, would you like a cup of tea?'

'Yes, please.' He realised it was the only thing he was likely to get from her. 'Could you possibly get me a glass of water as well? I'm very dry.'

'Of course. Do you have milk and sugar in your tea?'

'Milk but no sugar, thank you.'

'All right, I shan't be long.' She closed the door hurriedly and left, leaving Hugh to suspect that they might be hiding some horror from him. Of course, it was also possible that the nurse's hedging was simply an instance of the usual coyness associated with feminine matters.

The nurse returned quite soon with a cup of tea and a glass of water.

'Thank you,' he said. 'Look, I'm very anxious to know what's happening.' Irritatingly, his twitch took that as its cue, and he fought to control it.

'Of course you are, Mr Linthwaite, and someone will see you as soon as we have something to tell you.' She left before he could ask her anything further.

Hugh relieved the dryness in his mouth and was about to try the tea when the same nurse reappeared.

'Mr Linthwaite,' she said, 'they're taking your wife down to theatre but there's absolutely nothing to worry about. Mr Horsfall is going to perform a caesarean section. That means—'

'I know what a caesarean section is.' He was stunned for a second and then he asked, 'Don't I have to sign something before an operation?'

'No, Mrs Linthwaite has given her consent. You should go home and try to get some sleep. You can call in the morning and we'll have something to tell you.'

Hugh shook his head decisively. 'I couldn't possibly do that.'

'In that case, drink your tea and try not to worry.'

Hugh returned to his seat thinking how idiotic it was to tell someone not to worry, although nurses had no doubt been doing it since nursing began. It was an example of accepted silliness, like calling surgeons 'Mr', as if they were still barbers who sawed off limbs as a profitable side-line, and talking about 'performing' an operation. If only it were so simple. 'The theatre team will be joined by Mr Horsfall in a performance of the Caesarean Section in B Flat.' There was nothing simple about it, and particularly when the patient was Ellen.

The agony continued, during which Hugh re-examined every square inch of the bare waiting room. In his mind, he catalogued the empty picture rail, the beige-distempered walls, the white tiles edged with green beneath them, the coves where the walls met the terrazzo floor, and above them the central lamp with its glass shade and the elaborate ceiling rose and cornice. He made himself repeat the process several times because it was the only distraction available to him. He had estimated the dimensions of the room and was about to calculate its cubic capacity when the door opened and a grey-haired man of middle years entered the room. His expression was calm but solemn.

'Mr Linthwaite?' He offered his hand. 'I'm Horsfall, consultant gynaecologist. Your wife is out of surgery now but still under anaesthetic. She's had an exhausting time and is very weak.'

Hugh's heart was pounding so that he could barely speak. 'Will she survive?'

'She's lost rather a lot of blood but if she is allowed to rest she should make a full recovery in time.'

'And the baby?'

For the first time Mr Horsfall looked uncomfortable. 'I'm sorry, Mr Linthwaite, we were unable to save the infant. It was stillborn.'

Hugh took in the news slowly. 'What was it, girl or boy?'

'Do you really want to know that?'

'I wouldn't ask you if I didn't want to know.'

'Very well, Mr Linthwaite, it was a girl.'

Hugh was silent. Jane Louise Victoria had emerged from the womb lifeless. She would know none of the experiences he and Ellen had planned for her. Those months of anticipation had culminated in total loss.

'I'm very sorry, Mr Linthwaite.'

Hugh heard him only vaguely. He had seen death a thousand times and had to accept it. He'd honoured the dead and concentrated his concern for the moment on the survivors. On this occasion, however, the sole survivor was the woman who meant everything to him. He asked, 'When can I see my wife?'

'My advice to you is to go home now and rest. Tomorrow, after rounds, at ten o'clock would be a good time to visit her.'

'May I look in now?'

Mr Horsfall shook his head. 'I don't advise it. She's still recovering from the anaesthetic and is very weak, as I told you earlier. Come back in the morning.'

It was difficult advice to take but Hugh had no choice but to trust the professionals. He offered his hand and said, 'Thank you for everything, Mr Horsfall.'

* * *

When he opened his eyes the morning light was penetrating the room through a gap between the curtains. He had slept for only a little while and his eyes and mouth felt dry. He spent a few seconds adjusting to wakefulness and then, as suddenly and as painfully as a stab wound, the events of the night came back to him and he closed his eyes tightly as he recalled his conversation with Mr Horsfall. With an effort he dispelled the memory. He had to think about Ellen. She would be distraught. He had to see her. He focused his sleep-blurred eyes on the bedside clock and saw that the time was five-and-twenty minutes past seven. He must have slept for about three hours, and now he must get up. He would buy some chrysanthemums to take to the hospital. Ellen loved chrysanthemums, and he was determined to indulge her in every way he could.

Two-and-a-half hours later he arrived at Cullington General Hospital with a dozen gold, yellow and cream chrysanthemums pleasingly arranged for him by a sympathetic florist's assistant, and a bag containing Ellen's nightwear and sponge bag. The Head Porter directed him to Ward Seven and advised him to call in the first instance at Sister's office. Sister Campbell, he informed him, was 'a holy terror and a stickler for discipline,' but Hugh was too preoccupied to be impressed by his warning. He took the Head Porter's directions and located Sister's office. Through the glass-panelled door he could see Mr Horsfall in conversation with an ample and serious woman in a severe, navy-blue uniform. Mr Horsfall was drinking tea. Hugh tapped on the glass and the woman opened the door. He was about to introduce himself, when Mr Horsfall saved him the trouble.

'Sister,' he said, 'this is Mr Linthwaite.'

'How do you do?' Sister Campbell eyed Hugh as she might regard an unmade bed and said, 'If you give me those flowers I'll have them put into water.'

'Thank you.'

'You may see your wife for a few minutes and then she must rest.'

'Very well.'

'It's important that you don't let her see you're worried. It would upset her.'

'I've no doubt it would, Sister, but I'd still like to see her.'

Before she could reply, Mr Horsfall said, 'Sister, I'd appreciate a quick word with Mr Linthwaite before he sees his wife.'

'Of course, sir.' She left the office, taking the chrysanthemums with her.

'I shan't keep you above a few minutes, Mr Linthwaite,' said the surgeon, 'but I must speak to you before I go.'

Hugh stiffened, wondering if Ellen had maybe suffered a relapse. 'What do you want to speak to me about?'

Mr Horsfall looked down at the floor and then directly at Hugh. 'I'm sorry I had to give you such awful news last night, Mr Linthwaite, particularly as I'm afraid I have more. Basically, I have to warn you that it would be most inadvisable for Mrs Linthwaite ever to become pregnant again.'

Hugh realised he'd been holding his breath. He released it impatiently and said, 'My dear fellow, do you really imagine I'd put her through all that a second time?'

Mr Horsfall looked shamefaced. 'No, I don't,' he said, 'but it was my duty to warn you all the same.' He opened the office door as Sister Campbell returned, and said, 'Sister, will you take Mr Linthwaite to see his wife?'

'Of course, sir.'

Hugh thanked Mr Horsfall and followed her along the corridor, hoping she would resist the urge to restate the painfully obvious. It seemed to be common practice, at least for Horsfall and her. All Hugh wanted was to see Ellen.

Sister Campbell stopped outside a closed door. 'Just a few minutes,' she said, turning the handle and pushing the door open. 'Mrs Linthwaite,' she said in a softer tone, 'your husband is here.'

Uncertainly, because he had no idea what to expect, he entered the room and found not the woman he knew so well but one infinitely more delicate and helpless. She looked drained; in fact she looked awful, but she managed a weak smile until he bent to kiss her, and then tears formed copiously in her eyelids. 'I'm sorry,' she mumbled. 'I lost the baby.'

'Don't say that,' he told her gently. 'It wasn't your fault. It was no one's fault, just a tragic accident.' He drew the visitor's chair away from the wall and sat down, taking her hands between his. 'We'll get through this awful time, believe me, but the most important thing now is for you to get well again.' He gave her the handkerchief from his breast pocket to stem her tears, because to see her like that was torment. In an effort to lighten the mood for them both, he said, 'That means doing exactly as the staff here tell you, and I'm afraid that includes Sister Campbell.' He shuddered theatrically. 'You know, it's my belief that if we'd had her at the Front in nineteen-fourteen the Boche would have been terrified into submission long before Christmas.' His observation brought a smile to her face and that made him feel a little better too. 'And the other thing you have to remember is that I love you. Whatever else may happen, that simple truth is carved in stone.' He kissed her again, and a throat-clearing noise from the doorway re-alerted his sense of propriety.

'It's time to go, Mr Linthwaite. Your wife must rest.'

'Of course she must.' Hugh stood up and realised immediately that the chrysanthemums had magically reappeared in a vase on the window sill. Ellen had also seen them and, in her weakened state, still managed to register her delight.

Hugh waved to her from the doorway. 'Remember what I told you.'

He was rewarded with a smile.

As they came to Sister's office an idea came to him. 'Sister,' he said, 'the florist gave me a card with the flowers. I wasn't going to use it but I think I'd rather like to. Of course, that's if you don't mind seeing that it's delivered to my wife.'

Sister Campbell gave him a sharp look. 'We have more important things to do than to run all over the hospital delivering cards for forgetful husbands, Mr Linthwaite.'

'Ah, but this is more important than you think. This card could be instrumental in my wife's recovery.' He took the card and his fountain pen from his inside pocket and wrote his message.

To my beloved wife.
Rest and grow strong again.
'For where thou art, there is the world itself....'
All my love, Hugh.

'Ask one of your nurses to take this to her bedside and you'll be party to a minor miracle,' he told her.

'You're making a mockery of hospital discipline, Mr Linthwaite.' She nevertheless took the card from him.

Discipline, Sister? Two years ago I spent some time in Beckett Park Military Hospital, where patients are at the mercy of Queen Alexandra's Imperial Military Nursing Service, the very embodiment of discipline. By comparison, you are sweetness itself.'

There was the merest suggestion of a smile on her lips as she said, 'You may visit your wife again this evening if you wish. I suggest at between six and seven o'clock.'

'Thank you, Sister.' He left her and followed the signs to the exit, grieving for his lost child and no less anxious for Ellen's life, but with an air so neutral that no one, including Sister Campbell, would ever have gauged the depth of his feelings.

33

'Why are we here, Paul? That's not a philosophical question. I'm just wondering why you've brought me to a store that sells kitchen equipment.' Plum unfastened her seat belt, thankful at least that she was a passenger for once, with the catch conveniently on her right.

'You were telling me how frustrating it is that so many jobs in the kitchen call for two hands.'

'Yes, it drives me round the bend.'

'So I've brought you to a place that has a range of tools for the appendicularly challenged.'

'The what?'

'Those who have a missing or malfunctioning limb.'

She stepped out of the car and closed the door. 'That's a new one on me.'

'I found it last night on the internet,' he told her proudly.

'There must be a name for people who search the web for new words.'

'If there is,' he assured her, 'it'll be on the web.'

Paul held the shop door open for Plum and for two women who walked past him talking animatedly. 'It's my pleasure,' he told them. One of them gave him a questioning look before returning to their conversation.

'It's a myth, what they say about multi-tasking,' he told Plum. 'Thanking me for my act of courtesy was a job too many for those two.'

'I think you've just got to blame poor manners for that.'

Paul looked disappointed. 'Just when I thought I was beginning to understand female psychology,' he said, leading her to the shelves where tools for the disabled and disadvantaged were displayed.

'Something I've wondered about,' said Plum, 'is that you never talk much about your time with Diane. I feel quite guilty, having given you chapter and verse of my past.' She picked up a battery-powered can opener and examined it. It looked very much like the one she had.

'We weren't together for very long,' he said, 'thirteen years, that's all.'

'Even so, you don't talk about her very much.'

'That's because so many things have happened since then. I'm not making light of the years we were married; I wouldn't trade them for anything. I'm just saying that since Diane died twenty years ago I've had to get on with my life, and that's created lots of new experiences.'

'Have you never thought of re-marrying?' Grateful though she was to Paul for the gesture, she didn't find kitchen stores at all stimulating. Conversation was much more appealing.

'No.' He appeared to be looking for something among the shelves. 'I've had my moments, not that I'd be indelicate enough to talk about them, but I've never set out to get married again and I've never made a point of avoiding it either. It just hasn't happened.' With a look of triumph, he held up a tong-like device and said, 'This is what I was looking for.'

'It looks like one of those forceps they use to deliver reluctant babies,' she said, mentally crossing her legs.

'It's for picking up large jars and cans with one hand,' he told her.

'You know, that could be very useful.' She squinted at the price tag on the shelf.

'Nine-fifty.'

'Thank you, Paul. I really should wear my glasses.'

'You should,' he agreed. 'You could get so much more out of life.'

'So says the man who trawls the internet for new words.'

He seemed not to hear her but continued instead to search the shelves without apparent success. Eventually, he said, 'Did you discuss that matter with your doctor?'

'Yes, he advised me to think about it for a little longer, a sort of cooling-off period, before going ahead.'

'That sounds fair enough.'

'It'll make no difference. I'm still going to have it done.'

'You make it sound like double-glazing.'

She nodded. 'That's how I feel about it. It's a practical expedient.' She put down the one-handed tray she'd been inspecting. 'You know,' she said with an amused smile, 'he told me the oddest thing. Apparently, I'll need to learn to walk again. The two arms help the body to balance, you see. Take one away and....' She inclined her head towards the floor.

'That could be interesting. I imagine you'll have physiotherapy after it.'

'I should think so. There's so much support nowadays, we rather take it for granted.' She was thinking of some letters she'd found that morning. They'd seldom been far from her thoughts. 'Do you remember my telling you about some letters I'd found from a girl, one of Aunt Ellen's violin pupils?'

'The girl who won a scholarship, yes, I remember.'

'I found another this morning, a letter of sympathy expressed in general terms, but that's not all. I found another letter, a rather more detailed one. As far as I can make out, it's from the girl's mother. She offers her sympathy on the stillbirth and makes reference to her sister having had a caesarean section too.'

'That really was a bundle of misfortune.'

'Yes, poor Aunt Ellen must have had an awful time, especially when you consider how things must have been in hospitals in those days.'

'I daresay Hugh suffered too.'

'I'm sure he did, and it tells me something else as well; something that very likely gave rise to one of those accusations my wretched Uncle Joseph made about them. The letters are dated September and the wedding was in March. My guess was right.'

He nodded. 'They rang the bell.'

'Yes, and that time I went to see Uncle Hugh, you know, that dreadful Easter holiday I told you about, I could have spoken to him about my problem. It wouldn't have solved it but at least I'd have had a sympathetic listener when I needed one most.'

'It's all in the past. But listen, if that's all you're going to buy, we may as well go to the checkout now and then I'll buy you a wet and a wad in the café.'

'A what and a what?' It was a day of translation.

'A cup of tea and a sandwich, a cake, a pastry or whatever appeals to you.'

'That's a welcome suggestion. You must be sick to death of hearing about surgery.'

'Oh, it's not the first time I've been down that path.'

'Isn't it?'

'You asked me about Diane earlier. She had a double mastectomy.'

'Oh, Paul.' She put her hand on his arm. 'I'm so sorry. I really have been horribly insensitive.'

'You weren't to know, but at least you can be confident now that I'm not squeamish about surgery.'

'Listen Paul,' she said, 'I'll get the tea. It's high time I did my share of the listening.'

34

The improvement in Ellen's health and state of mind following the operation was a huge relief for Hugh, who had been able to think of nothing else, and could now plan ahead. Rosen had found him a number of solo engagements during Ellen's pregnancy, and now Hugh was able to report that Ellen would be available again in a matter of weeks.

'It will be business as usual,' said Ellen cheerfully.

'But you must be careful.'

'Don't fuss. You sound like Sister Campbell.'

'Hardly. For one thing, I haven't an Edinburgh accent.'

Ellen laughed. 'Yourr husband is a rremarrkable man, Mrs Linthwaite,' she mimicked.

'I hope you told her you already knew that.'

'Of course I did. Only you would think of quoting Shakespeare on a florist's card. It was Shakespeare, wasn't it?'

'*Henry the Sixth, Part Two,*' he confirmed.

'Sister Campbell brought it to me shortly after you left. She propped it up against my water jug so that I could see it easily. I kept falling asleep and then waking up and reading it, and I'm sure each time I read it I felt better.' She took his hand and squeezed it. 'Whatever made you think of it?'

'It was desperation. I couldn't find the words I wanted so I fell back on the Bard and he came up trumps as usual.'

She picked up the card and examined it again. 'It's unfinished, though, isn't it?'

'It's a long play.'

'Oh Hugh, don't tease. I mean it's only one line. What comes next?'

'I don't know. It can't be anything important.' Hurriedly changing the subject, he picked up a circular cake tin and as he prised off the lid he said, 'Mrs Naylor's been spoiling me and she'll do the same for you when you come home. Meanwhile, she's baked you a fruit cake.' He inclined the tin to show her. 'She thought you might like to share it with a few people here.'

'Well, I'm certainly not going to eat it all by myself.' She inhaled appreciatively. 'It smells delicious. You'll thank her for me, won't you?'

'Of course I will, but you could do that yourself. I've arranged for her to come this evening.'

'Oh lovely. Thank you, darling. She's been so understanding about things.'

He laughed. 'Do you mean dates that don't add up?'

'Yes, that's just what I mean. She might well have disapproved but she's never so much as hinted at it.'

'That could be because she's trodden the same path.'

'Has she?'

'We were training in Hampshire when Naylor came to me and requested compassionate leave. I put his request to the Commanding Officer and the whole sad story came out, so we bundled him off to Yorkshire so that he could tie the knot.'

She tried to make sense of what he was telling her. 'But Mrs Naylor has no children,' she said.

'She suffered a miscarriage. We were at the Front by that time, so Naylor was unable to go home to see her. He was killed a few days later.' He added, 'That was one of the reasons I felt so sorry for her when she came looking for work.'

'Well, I'm glad you were able to help her, and not just because she looks after us so well.' She sniffed at the cake again before replacing the lid, and said, 'I suppose I should learn how to do some cooking. I mean if Mrs Naylor were ever ill, for example, we'd have to cope then.'

'There may well come a time when servants are a thing of the past,' he said, 'at least for most people. The war's made a huge difference to the number in service and now, with unrest up and down the country, none of us knows how things will be in ten or twenty years' time.'

'Yes,' she reflected, 'I don't think Mr Asquith is going to return to power now.'

'Was he your last hope for the future?'

'He's an honest man,' she said, 'and where there's honour there's always hope, even when the political system is dominated by men.'

'That great-aunt of yours really left her mark.'

'Yes, she did, as a matter of fact. She had the courage of her convictions.'

'Heaven help us,' he said, making a tragic face, 'when women start interfering in politics.'

'Hugh,' she warned, 'you're teasing me again. At least, I hope you are.'

He gave the game away by smiling. It was enough for him that she was well enough to be teased.

35

Plum remembered Gledhill's Music Shop from her childhood. It was a familiar sight in Cullington then and, whilst the shop was no longer owned by the Gledhill family, its owners had kept the name so that there was a pleasing sense of continuity about the place.

'Do you need any help?' A girl, maybe in her late teens asked the question. She wore a lapel badge, which Plum could read now that she was wearing her glasses. It said, 'I Got My Grade 8.' Plum was very pleased for her.

'Yes, I'd like some help, please. I'm looking for a tutor book suitable for a child of ten and I'm a little out of touch because it's been rather a long time since I taught beginners.'

'Right, so you've done some teaching, then? You see, some teachers who, like, know what they're doing just use pieces and, like, explain it as they go. It just depends on how much you know.'

'I imagine it does,' agreed Plum. She noticed that a man of more mature years had caught her eye and was heading her way. He seemed to recognise her.

'Excuse me,' he said, 'aren't you Victoria Linthwaite?'

'That's right.'

'I'm Tony Enright, the Manager here. I'm really pleased to meet you, Miss Linthwaite.' Turning to the bemused assistant, he said, 'Mel, this is the pianist Victoria Linthwaite. You sold one of her CDs this morning.'

'I'm gratified to hear it,' said Plum. 'Don't worry,' she told the girl, 'you weren't to know.'

'Mel,' said Mr Enright, 'they need some help in the CD Department. Go and give them a hand, please.'

'Right.' The girl disappeared, embarrassed and no doubt grateful to be out of the way.

'She's a new Saturday girl,' Mr Enright told Plum. 'She'll get the hang of it in time. Meanwhile, how can I help?'

'I need some material for a beginner. It's my granddaughter and she's ten. I last taught a beginner thirty-some years ago, so I'm rather feeling my way.'

'All right, maybe a tutor book is the answer. Your granddaughter will be able to look at all the things you've taught her. You'll still be able to do it your way, but she'll have something she can refer to when she's alone.'

'That sounds very sensible.' Plum ran her eye over the books on the display rack and was surprised to find an old friend among the books of pieces. '*Scenes at a Farm*,' she said. 'That's the one I started on.' She turned the pages, remembering the pieces she'd played more than fifty years earlier. 'Mind you,' she said, 'teachers were stricter and more demanding in those days. I certainly wouldn't start my granddaughter on anything as advanced as this, and I take your point, Mr Enright. A tutor book would be much more suitable.'

They looked at several tutors until Plum found one she liked. It was intelligently written and the pieces were attractive. She paid for it and left Mr Enright to tell the rest of his staff about his latest customer. It was an uncomfortable feeling, knowing as she did that the CDs they were selling represented her swansong as a performing pianist.

She looked briefly in the window of Stevenson's bakery. Their bread looked far more appetising than the mass-produced kind she usually bought, so she went into the shop and bought a large white bloomer. Then, as she was leaving, she spotted Paul across the road. He'd also seen her and he crossed over as soon as he could.

'Hello Plum,' he said, 'where are you bound?'

'I'm on my way home. I've got everything I came for.'

'Where are you parked?'

'In the car park at the bottom of Northgate.'

'Same here. I'll walk with you. Actually, I have to go into the Victoria Arcade first, to the fishmonger there.'

'Is he special?'

'I suppose he is. You get to know the tradesmen you can trust, and he's always looked after me.'

Plum gave a theatrical sigh. 'I have so much to learn,' she said.

'But think of how much you've learned already.'

'I suppose I have picked up quite a lot. Of course, it helps to have a knowledgeable neighbour.'

'That goes without saying.'

They walked through the glass-roofed arcade to the fishmonger's, where Paul bought smoked haddock and prawns. 'It's for fish pie,' he told Plum. 'If you like, I'll show you how to make it.'

'That's an offer I can't refuse. I like fish pie.'

As they walked away from the fishmonger's stall, he said, 'I have something else to put to you.'

'Oh?'

'Would you consider coming to a dance at the Wool Exchange Club next Saturday evening? They have them regularly. I've been to a few and they were very good. There's an excellent live band that plays music from an age when quality abounded. I know it's different from the kind of music you're used to but I'm sure you'll enjoy it.'

The invitation was so unexpected that Plum had to think quickly. She'd not been to a dance for a very long time but, whilst it wasn't the kind of thing she would normally think of doing, Paul had shown her so much kindness she felt it would be churlish to turn him down. 'It sounds rather grand,' she said, 'and yes, I'd like that very much. I'd no idea you were a member there.'

'Yes, I joined when I was doing some publicity work for the band when it was starting out. The leader and I are old friends and he and his wife have asked if we'll join them at their table. He told me when I saw him just now that he's very keen to meet you.'

'Him as well?' Plum told him about the man in the music shop.

'They call it the price of fame, don't they? Forever being recognised by members of the public? I daresay you'll have heard of our host too. His name's Frank Morrison.'

Wheels turned and clicked into place in Plum's mind. 'Not Frank Morrison the composer?'

'That's right.'

'Paul, you've been holding out on me. You might have said so earlier. Someone told me he lived close by, now I think of it.'

'He does. He's just a son of Cullington like the rest of us.'

'I'd still like to meet him. By the way, what's everyone wearing?'

'Party frocks. According to Frank, they keep their long ball gowns for big occasions such as Christmas and the Midsummer Ball. They have a dance almost every month and I imagine no woman wants to be seen in the same thing too often.'

'Well, I've really no idea what I'm going to wear, but I'm looking forward to it already.'

* * *

It wasn't the only invitation Plum received that week. Two days later Malcolm phoned, offering her lunch at the Italian restaurant in Westgate.

It was an excellent meal and they had plenty to talk about. Family developments and the events of the past several years occupied the first two courses.

'The cheesecake is definitely out as far as I'm concerned,' said Plum, eyeing the dessert trolley.

'Why?'

'It's loaded with calories.'

Malcolm was amused. 'You don't look like someone who needs to worry about calories,' he said.

'Oh, but I must. It's only by avoiding cheesecake and similar temptations that I can stay like this.' In the end, she settled for the lemon tart, telling herself that the pastry crust was quite thin.

Malcolm ordered for them both and said, 'I've been thinking about that thing you were talking about last time we met, the Uncle Hugh business. You know, I'd never really thought much about him before now, but talking with you brought things back to me that I'd completely forgotten, and I think I can tell you the source of the lion's share of the unpleasantness, and very likely the reason for it.'

'I'm intrigued. Do go on.'

'Well, I told you about my father's attitude towards him and Aunt Ellen, but his prejudice was all second-hand. The original villain, as I remember, was my grandfather.'

'On the Linthwaite side of the family?'

'Yes, Sidney Linthwaite.'

The waitress arrived with their desserts and Plum demonstrated her resolve again by choosing not to have cream on hers. She was also impatient to hear what Malcolm had to tell her.

'As you know, my family had a holding in a leather goods manufacturing company until my father died and the shares were sold, but what you may not know is that at one time my grandfather and his father owned the entire company. It's quite surprising really, because I've often thought that those two should never have gone into business.'

Plum couldn't help being impatient. 'But where did Uncle Hugh and Aunt Ellen come into it?'

'Ah, well, back in the early twenties there was a cash-flow problem. They'd overstretched themselves in their investment in raw materials and machinery and were desperate for liquidity, so my grandfather called on Uncle Hugh to see if he could interest him in buying up some of the company's unissued stock.'

'But Uncle Hugh wasn't a wealthy man. The money was Aunt Ellen's.'

'That's right, and the visit turned out to be fruitless. I don't know exactly what was said on that day, but for some reason my grandfather blamed him for all the ills that befell the company thereafter.'

'It's not my place to criticise your grandfather but I must say I'm not impressed so far.'

'Neither was anyone else. He was a most unappealing man. He was also completely unprincipled. My mother couldn't stand him.'

'And was that really the reason for all that spitefulness?'

'It was the start of it. The company had eventually to accept a takeover bid from Fur Traders Limited, which meant that my family lost control of the business, and my grandfather's grudge against Uncle Hugh grew into an obsession.'

'And it's not difficult to imagine him using any scrap of gossip to harm them both in the eyes of the family and in any way he could.' The picture in Plum's mind was now complete....

The unpleasantness Malcolm had described to her lingered in her mind for some time after their lunchtime meeting but Nicola's visit that evening provided the perfect antidote. Her first piano lesson was all that Plum had expected: a heady mixture of wonder and achievement. Success, that latecomer to Nicola's life, was now a small but growing feature in it.

'I had to read to Mr Zachary,' she said.

'Wonderful!' Clearly, excitement was in order. 'Who's Mr Zachary?'

'He's the head teacher. He said I'd made excellent progress and he wished you were a teacher in his school.'

'Heaven forbid.'

'And Mrs Holroyd told the class about that thing I've got so they don't think it's weird.' She wrinkled her nose and added, 'Well, they still think it's a bit weird. They keep knocking on desks and things and asking me what colour it is, but Mrs Holroyd says they'll soon get bored with it.'

'I'm sure they will.'

'And everybody's been asking me where I had my hair cut.' The development had evidently taken her by surprise.

'So the other girls like it?'

'Most of them. There's one or two who are not very nice.'

'There always are,' said Plum. 'And what about the boys? Do they like it?'

She wriggled self-consciously. 'There's one. Drew says he likes it. He always used to stick up for me when the others were getting at me.'

'Boys like him are worth their weight in gold,' said Plum. 'They usually grow into nice people as well.'

With her customary suddenness Nicola changed the subject and asked, 'Have you found out anything more about Uncle Hugh and Auntie Ellen?'

'Yes, I had lunch with Uncle Malcolm today and he told me something that shocked me.' She gave her the outline of their conversation and saw the child's face fill with indignation.

'So that old man caused all the trouble?'

'He was a young man when it began.' Plum had no idea why she said that, unless it was that keeping track of the generations had become a habit.

'Well, I think somebody should have said something,' said Nicola, with at least thirty years' disgruntlement in her tone.

'I'm inclined to agree, Nicola.'

'Have you read all the letters now?' She seemed concerned that Plum might have done it in her absence.

'Not all of them. I've read a few since I saw you last.' She told her as gently as she could about the stillborn child and the caesarean section, and Nicola surprised her by telling her that one of her classmates had been born by caesarean. She was predictably saddened by the stillbirth.

'There's one thing I've been putting off reading,' said Plum, 'and it's the order of service for Aunt Ellen's funeral. She died in nineteen sixty-eight. I was seventeen at the time and I knew nothing about it, so it's particularly sad for me.'

Nicola made her decision promptly. 'I don't want to look at it either. I want to remember her in that photo.'

'In that case,' said Plum with some relief, 'I've got an important task for you. I'm going to a dance on Saturday with Mr Watson – yes, it was quite a surprise – and I want you to look at some dresses with me and tell me which you like best.'

36

In the end Plum and Nicola decided unanimously on the dark-purple dress with the silver border motif, a choice that Paul endorsed enthusiastically when he arrived to take her out to the waiting taxi.

The Wool Exchange was an entirely new experience for her. Captivated, she took Paul's arm and together they climbed the wide, marble staircase lined with the imposing portraits of centuries of prominent clothiers. Even when Cullington had previously been her home she had never had occasion to enter the building but had regarded it somewhat diffidently as a grand and exclusive monument to the town's past. On entering the ballroom, however, she was impressed in a different and infinitely more welcoming way. In contrast to the marble Regency pillars and grand features of the ground floor, it was furnished in the Art Deco style, and Plum imagined the original design must have been carefully preserved to retain the impression of warmth and conviviality that was immediately apparent. The chandeliers, the drape curtains and scallop-fronted bandstand completed a picture that she found quite entrancing.

'It's lovely, Paul,' she said. 'I never imagined it would look like this.'

'When the band was formed twenty-three years ago, the original glory of the place was rather faded,' he told her. 'It was having the band and the regular dances that prompted the committee to get the decorators in, and that made my job much more rewarding.' He caught someone's eye and said, 'Here's Frank. Oh, and there's Sarah too.'

Plum saw a grey-haired, solidly-built man now joined by a tall, attractive woman maybe in her mid-to-late forties. She wore a light-blue dress with elbow-length bell sleeves.

'Frank and Sarah,' said Paul, greeting them in turn, 'I'd like you to meet Victoria, known to her friends as "Plum".'

Plum shook hands with them both, saying, 'It's very kind of you to invite us. Thank you very much.'

'It really is our pleasure,' said Frank. 'I must leave you very briefly, just to get things started, but Sarah will take you to our table. What would you both like to drink, by the way?'

They opted for dry white wine.

'That makes it easy,' said Frank. 'Leave it with me.' He took his leave of them, stopping to speak to a steward as he made for the band room.

'They'll bring the wine to us,' said Sarah. 'It's actually bar service only but they bend the rules for Frank.' Turning to Plum, she said, 'Frank's been like an excited schoolboy all day. "I never realised," he said, "Victoria Linthwaite's been living next door to Paul Watson all this time".'

'Just three months,' said Plum, 'and I hope he won't be too disappointed to hear that I don't play any longer.'

'Yes, we know that and we were very sorry to hear it.'

'Thank you.' Plum was distracted by the faint sound of instruments tuning.

A steward came to the table with an ice bucket containing a bottle of Pinot Grigo in one hand and a tray of wine glasses in the other. As he left them, Plum saw the musicians taking their places on the bandstand. When they were settled, there was a round of applause as Frank walked on and the band went straight into their signature number, which Plum recognised but couldn't name. All the same it felt spontaneous and exciting.

'Twenty-three years on, Frank and I still get a buzz when they play that,' Sarah told them. 'It's a number the Ambrose orchestra used to play: "The Sun Has Got His Hat On".'

The short number ended to more applause and Frank turned to the members and their guests.

'Good evening, ladies and gentlemen. On behalf of the New Albion Dance Orchestra, let me welcome you to the Exchange Club Ballroom. It's good to see so many of you here. Let's begin the evening with a waltz by that master of melody Eric Coates: "By the Sleepy Lagoon".'

As the music began, Sarah said, 'You two go and dance. Frank'll come down and join us after this number.'

Paul hesitated. 'Are you sure?'

'Absolutely.'

He offered Plum his hand. 'May I have the pleasure?'

'By all means.'

As they joined the line of dance Plum said, 'That sailor who taught you did a good job.'

Paul shook his head. 'No, I was hopeless until I met a steward from one of the cruise liners and he refined my technique. He was as camp as a boy scout's bugle but an excellent dancer.'

'What an unusual life you've led, Paul.'

'No stranger than yours.'

'Perhaps not.' They danced on without speaking. Paul seemed to be enjoying it, and Plum certainly was. When the number ended they applauded the band and returned to the table.

Sarah asked, 'Have you two danced together before?'

'Only once, in my kitchen,' Paul told her.

She showed no surprise, but said, 'You look good on the floor.'

'Thank you.'

Frank was introducing the pianist, who would be acting as bandleader for most of the evening, and then the band launched into a quickstep. In a very short time, he re-joined them at the table and poured the wine. 'Tell me if I'm wrong, Plum,' he said, 'but didn't we meet briefly at the College?'

'I think we did, at a party. I remember there was an ornamental post horn in the house where the party was held, and someone bet you a pound you couldn't play the *Post Horn Galop* on it.'

'Oh dear.' Frank covered his face with his hands. 'I must have been plastered.'

'Plastered or not, you managed it. I was so impressed I've followed your career ever since.'

'Bless you, Plum. Some good came of that bet after all.'

Sarah was confused. 'Is it really "Galop" or "Gallop"?'

'It was originally "Galop",' Frank told her, recovering from his embarrassment, 'but the name's been used and misused over the years.'

'I was thinking of the mail-coach connection.'

'Sarah taught dance and various things at what used to be Beckworth College,' he explained. That's what she was doing when we met. It was also around the time we set up the band. What a drama that was.'

Paul was quick to ask, 'You and Sarah or the band?'

'Both, as it happened.' Sarah was happy to clear up that point.

'It's time for a slow foxtrot,' said the pianist. 'We're going to play "Deep Purple" and here to sing it for us is Jake.'

'He's quite good,' said Sarah before turning to Frank and asking, 'Are you going to dance with me and remind me why I fell for you all those years ago?'

Frank stood up and took her hand.

'Shall we join them, Plum?' Paul was already on his feet.

As they danced, she said, 'They talk about the formation of the band as if it happened yesterday.'

'It was very big in their lives at the time. Naturally, they'll be able to tell you more than I can. They just brought me in to make a video, take some pictures and put a brochure together.'

Plum listened for a while and said, 'The singer's pretty good, isn't he?'

'He's quite good, but you should have heard Dan, who sang with the original band.'

'You're beginning to sound like them.'

'Sorry.'

'Don't be. Just enjoy yourself.'

Paul gave an exaggerated sigh. 'I'm enjoying every minute. I have the company of friends, chilled wine, the best dance music and a lovely partner.'

Plum merely smiled and squeezed the hand that was holding hers.

When they all met again at the table, Frank said, 'I think I must have been a year or so ahead of you at the College, Plum, now I think of it.'

'I was there from 'sixty-nine.'

'Ah, I was there from 'sixty-seven to seventy. I had to leave a year early.'

Plum nodded sympathetically. 'Me too.'

Sarah asked, 'Shall we go and leave these two together, Paul? They've so much in common it's a shame not to.'

'Maybe we should talk about something else,' said Plum. 'I'm fascinated by what you've both said so far about the band. How did it all happen?'

'Basically, it was a phoenix,' said Frank. 'My daughter Kate and I arrived here one Sunday morning, expecting the usual orchestra rehearsal, only to find that the long-threatened breakaway orchestra had been formed. We found the casualties in this ballroom: a dozen or so very dejected and rejected old men. Kate was heartbroken when she saw them – she was only nineteen – and, if I'm honest, I still find the image disturbing.'

'But why were they left out?'

'*Anno Domini*. They'd reached the age when mistakes were more frequent and memory was less reliable.'

'The leader of the pack was seventy-five. I know that because he was my granddad,' Sarah told her, 'not that I ever called him that. I had to call him "Hutch", as his friends all did. He couldn't bear to be called "Granddad".'

Plum could understand that.

'Hutch was my oldest friend,' said Frank, 'and I was going through a bit of a crisis at the time, but I had to do something.' He added quickly, 'Not that it was all down to me. Others became involved.'

'You were the hero of the hour,' said Sarah, stroking his hand, 'and the band was your idea.'

'I don't suppose there are many of the original members left,' said Plum.

'Just Frank and I,' said Sarah, 'and Kate when she's here. Oh, and there was the singer Dan. He was around Kate's age.'

'Norman was the last of the old guard to go,' said Frank. 'We thought he was indestructible but he died three years ago at ninety-five.'

'And Hutch died five years ago,' said Sarah.

The pianist announced another slow foxtrot, and Frank said, 'Let's all stop talking about the dear departed and cheer ourselves up. Paul, do you mind if I ask Plum to dance?'

'Be my guest. Shall we join them, Sarah?'

Plum began to apologise for her useless arm, but Frank said, 'Rest it on mine the way you did with Paul.'

'Thank you. I'm afraid my disability is still new enough for me to feel awkward about it.'

'There's nothing awkward about you. Try to put it from your mind.'

'I'll try. It shouldn't be too difficult, because I can't help thinking about those poor old men we've been talking about. They must have been devastated.'

'They were,' agreed Frank. 'It hit most of them very hard but they were made of stern stuff, as they say. Most of them had come through a depression and a war, and when they were over the initial shock they soon came bouncing back.'

'You have to admire that kind of resilience. They were a tough generation.'

'They were,' he agreed, 'but you don't have to go so far back to find it. There's an example at our table.'

There were only two possibilities. Plum waited to be told.

'You only have to consider Paul. He was going through an awful time when we met.'

'Do you mean with his wife's illness?'

'Yes, it was a horrible business, but Paul's a trouper and he came through in the end.'

It was a sobering message. Plum decided to change the subject to a more cheerful one. 'What are you working on now?'

'I'm just finishing the score of a two-part TV drama set during the First World War. It's to be screened next year to mark the hundredth anniversary of the war, and I've no doubt there'll be more to follow.'

'I'll look forward to that. I loved your *Daniel Defoe* score." I got it on CD and played it to death in the car.'

'Thank you for that, Plum. You've done much the same for me.' He checked himself and added, 'And not just me. My daughter Kate was playing with the Midland Philharmonic when you recorded the Chopin concertos. She loved them.'

'I'm glad.'

The evening continued to be enjoyable, especially when Sarah got up to sing 'Blue Moon.' It seemed to give Frank a lot of pleasure too, and Paul explained later that it was the first song Sarah had sung with the band in 1990. It must have been a heady time.

There was only one awkward moment, when Frank asked Plum directly if she had any plans to return one-handed to the platform. It was something that, with so much going on in her mind, she really didn't want to discuss.

37

Three weeks later Plum was recovering from her operation. To Heather's disapproval, she'd had it done privately. There was no doubt much to be said for Heather's point of view, but pain had been the ultimate dynamic in Plum's decision, and she could wait no longer.

She'd received a great deal of attention from visitors, so that she felt quite spoiled. She was only going to be in hospital for a few days, after all. Her visitors included Nigel and Heather, who were predictably and respectively awkward and correct, and Nicola, whose hugs and kisses said everything. Matthew made a flying visit, largely to thank her for his calculator, and Plum didn't mind as long as he refrained from listing the dubious benefits of the wretched implement.

Her principal visitor was Paul, who had also driven her to the hospital and who would drive her home when the time came. He arrived two days after the operation with a large tin of home-made biscuits.

'Paul,' she said, 'I'm very grateful but I'm supposed to be going home soon.'

'That's all right,' he said, 'I've made plenty, so you can share them round.'

'That could make me the most popular patient in the hospital.'

'So there's no problem. Have you seen Frank and Sarah? They said they were coming.'

'They came this morning. It was lovely to see them.' She waved him to a chair beside the bed. 'Do sit down, Paul, and stop worrying about me. I'm all right.' She knew what lay behind his fussing. He'd brought Diane into the same hospital and the association would always be there. 'How is little Henry?' She'd thought about him recently and, purely for Paul's benefit, his arm seemed a reasonable distraction from hers.

'He's going to have his plaster cast off next week.'

'Oh good. The poor little scrap was very frustrated.'

'He still talks about the piano lesson you gave him. They must be tired of hearing about it at school.'

She smiled. 'Like Nicola. She never talks about anything else.'

'Not even her great-great-great-aunt and uncle?'

'No, I think she's gone as far with them as she was ever going to, but they did her a power of good when she most needed it.'

'I think they did.'

She told him about her conversation with Nicola after the first piano lesson. 'There was something among those papers,' she said, 'that I was almost afraid to look at. It was the order of service for Aunt Ellen's funeral, and just the thought of it was too sad for words, but I did look at it eventually, and I'm glad I did.'

Paul nodded and waited.

'It was a very simple funeral, at least for its time. The most striking thing about it was a quotation that Uncle Hugh had handwritten on the back of the order of service. It said, "For where thou art, there is the world itself... And where thou art not, desolation."'

'I think we both have an idea of how he was feeling when he wrote that.'

'Yes, I think so too.'

'Do you know where he found it?'

'I suspect it's Shakespeare, but from what I've no idea, and that doesn't really matter. What it means to me is that those two had something very special going for them, something that Sidney Linthwaite and his side of the family couldn't even begin to imagine.'

Paul nodded. 'I think they've done you some good too,' he said.

'Yes, they have, and so has the evening at the Exchange Club. I keep thinking about it, you know.' It had been particularly good for her, as much as anything because her conversation with Frank had given her so much to think about.

'I'm glad. I knew you'd get something out of it.'

Something else was giving her cause for reflection as well, an item from her private collection of jumble acquired over forty or so years. Most of the things in it were keepsakes and souvenirs of various kinds but this was particularly special. It was a letter that Uncle Hugh had written to her shortly after their first meeting at her father's funeral. She found it such a comfort that she'd brought it into hospital to read at odd moments, and she took it out again when Paul had left.

Dear Vicky,

Thank you so much for your letter. Please accept my congratulations on winning the scholarship. I am more delighted than you can imagine, remembering as I do my feelings when I received similar news. It happened sixty years ago but the memory of it is as fresh as ever. Enjoy your success to the full; you've earned it.

And now I'm going to be presumptuous and offer you some avuncular advice. You clearly have a special gift and that is a wonderful thing. It's important, however, to remember that such a gift brings with it responsibility, in this case, to your audience. If that sounds particularly banal and obvious, let me tell you that there are still those who forget the fact from time to time, and who pay the penalty for it. No audience is less important than another, and an off-hand performance will always be remembered for quite the wrong reason. Equally, though, no audience is more loyal than one that has heard a memorable performance, and that's the kind that will help build your reputation. There'll be times when you'll feel dispirited or maybe under the weather, and it's for those occasions that nature provides adrenalin. I guarantee you'll feel better afterwards. There may be other times, of course, when the odds are completely against you, when you may encounter misfortune or tragedy, and then it will be up to you to find your way through it. When that happens, remember that there's an audience waiting to hear you, and they don't know about your troubles. They just want to hear the programme they've been promised, because they heard you once before and they know you won't let them down.

So much, then, for responsibility, because there also lies ahead of you the promise of a magnificent career that will give you more satisfaction than any other I can imagine, and I wish you well in it.

Please come and visit me whenever you wish, but do give me a call beforehand. I'm accepting rather less work now that I'm alone, but I want to be sure I'll be here when you come. In the meantime, take good care of yourself. I look forward very much to seeing you again.

Yours with great affection,
Your long-lost uncle,
Hugh.
P.S. The enclosed cheque is to help defray the cost of settling into your accommodation, another memory that sixty years have been unable to erase.

She folded the letter again and placed it on the top of her bedside cabinet. The whole exercise had been a fascinating experience that she wouldn't have missed for anything, but she felt the time had come to follow Nicola's example and leave Uncle Hugh and Aunt Ellen to enjoy the peace they both deserved.

38

April 1923

'Spring is always worth the wait,' said Ellen, taking Hugh's arm as they left the house. The walk across the park had become a regular habit when circumstances allowed, ever since her return from hospital in September, when a gentle daily stroll was not only advised but prescribed.

'It's been quite a wait,' said Hugh. 'This must be the first morning of the month when it hasn't rained.'

'You do exaggerate. Let's walk up Greenacre Road as far as one-hundred-and-fifty.'

'You're not thinking of moving back there, are you?'

'Of course not. I just want to look at it again and see the daffodils and crocuses in the park as we go.'

'I'm not sure about that,' said Hugh, sounding like a stern parent. 'You ask an awful lot, you know.'

'Indulge me this once.'

They walked on until the house gradually came into view. Then, after some thought, Ellen said, 'It doesn't look at all different.' She sounded disappointed.

'Do you feel it should?'

'Yes, now that it belongs to the new people it's more than likely assumed a completely new character.'

Hugh made field glasses with his hands and peered through them. 'My goodness,' he said, 'I do believe you're right.'

'What can you see?'

'Well, it's certainly taken a dislike to the morning room curtains, because it's changed them. I wish it hadn't taken the trouble, because the new ones are too awful for words.'

'Don't tease. I'll tell you what, though. The shrubs in the front garden have been trimmed, clipped, pruned or whatever the correct term is, because they look tidier than they have for ages.'

'The cheek of it.'

She squeezed his arm conspiratorially and asked, 'Do you remember that time we came back from... I think it was Manchester, and everyone was in bed so we hid behind the rhododendrons?'

'And you led me astray. I'll never forget it.'

'I did nothing of the kind, you wretched man.'

'Oh, don't misunderstand me. I'm glad you did, because I've never forgotten it even though so much has happened since then.'

'Yes, lots of good things as well as bad ones.'

They stood, remembering some of the lighter moments they'd spent together, until Hugh said, 'Shouldn't we be looking the other way?'

Confused for the moment, Ellen asked, 'At what?'

'Our home. That's where we need to concentrate our attention.'

'Yes, our future, of course.'

'Well, there is that, I suppose.'

'What else could you possibly have in mind?'

'I was thinking that the laurels and rhododendrons are in urgent need of pruning. I scent competition and I'm determined not to be outdone by the new people at one-fifty.'

'You're incorrigible.' It was the gentlest of rebukes, so mild it was almost a compliment.

They returned along the path between the daffodils and crocuses, now at peace, with the recent past easier to bear and the future beckoning once more.

39

Plum's hand was beginning to ache from the kind of use it hadn't known for more than two years, and she would soon need to rest it. She'd warmed up gradually, as she always had, and now it was time to warm down, beginning the process with the scale of D flat. In conversation with Frank Morrison she had learned that he shared her fondness for the key because of its richness and warmth, not that either of those qualities could currently be heard above the clatter of Paul's lawnmower. She was grateful to Paul, though, firstly for mowing her lawn and secondly for providing, however unwittingly, a camouflage of noise. She would have to admit to him sooner or later that he'd been right all along, but she wanted to prepare herself for the grand climb-down.

The moment came sooner than she had expected. She had just moved away from the piano when she became aware of coffee-making noises in her kitchen. A moment later Paul came into the room carrying a large envelope.

'Thank you, Paul,' she said. 'You've no idea how much I appreciate the jobs you do for me.'

'Oh, it's no trouble. It's a funny thing, though.'

'What is?' She thought he had that infuriating look men sometimes had when they were about to score a point.

'You know, I'll swear each time I came close to the house I could hear the piano.' He shook his head dismissively. 'It must have been my imagination.'

'Paul.'
'What?'
'Sit down.'
'Should we go into the kitchen? My gardening trousers are not exactly spotless.'
'They look clean enough to me.'
'All right.' He sank into his usual chair and waited with, from her point of view, exasperating patience for her to speak, which she finally did.

'You may as well know that I've started practising again. I'm also writing a right-hand arrangement of Paganini's Twenty-Fourth Caprice. I know I'm only doing what you've been nagging me to do, but I needed to make the decision in my own time. So there. And please take that self-satisfied smirk off your face.'

The grin remained undiminished. 'There's no self-satisfaction about it, Plum. I'm just delighted for your sake.'

'But you knew all along that it would happen. That's what's so infuriating.' She couldn't help smiling in spite of herself.

'No, that's where you're wrong. I always hoped it would happen, but that's different from knowing, and there were times you seemed so entrenched I was almost ready to give up.'

'I'll believe you. Did you know that Frank was going to appeal to my sense of shame?'

'I'd no idea at all. He told me about your conversation but it was news to me. Did it influence your decision?'

'The whole evening helped to some extent. The company, the atmosphere and being among musicians all contributed, I think. Certainly, the story of the band wasn't lost on me.'

'Good.' He sniffed the aroma coming from the kitchen. 'The coffee's ready.' He stood up. 'Shall we?'

They went through to the kitchen, where Paul poured coffee for them both. 'I'm glad that evening helped,' he said. 'I just wanted you to have a good time. The rest was a bonus.'

'I believe you, and it wasn't the only thing that swayed me.'
'No?'
'I was reminded of some advice I was given more than forty years ago. It was a timely reminder of something I should never have forgotten.'

'Well, it was obviously good advice.' He looked like a man who'd just remembered something. 'One moment,' he said, reaching for the envelope he'd brought into the house. 'This is for you. The sender wanted it delivered securely by hand.'

'How strange.' She turned it over. 'There's no return address.'

'Maybe you should open it.'

'It looks well-sealed. Would you mind?'

'This is one you really should open yourself, Plum.' He took out his pen knife and handed it to her. 'I'll hold it for you.'

'I scent a conspiracy,' she said, slitting open the gummed flap while Paul held the envelope. She pulled out a folder with a note attached.

Dear Plum,
Welcome back to the fold. I look forward to hearing you play this as part of a whole new repertoire.
Kind regards,
Frank.

'I don't believe it,' she said, opening the folder and reading aloud from the title page. ' "Concert Study in D Flat for the Right Hand, by Frank Morrison." ' From the opposite page she read to herself, *For Victoria Linthwaite.* Speechless for the moment, she looked across at Paul. Eventually, she asked, 'How on earth could he have known?'

'He was confident all along. He left it with me and asked me to give it to you at the right moment.'

'The scheming rogue…. I was right about the conspiracy,' she said, turning the pages, 'but I love the outcome, even if it does look infernally difficult.' She put it down to pick up her coffee and looked across at Paul. 'You're still looking pleased with yourself,' she said. 'What else have you got up your sleeve?'

'I just wondered if a celebration might be in order.'

'Oh, I daresay.'

'There's a new bistro just opened in the High Street.'

'Yes, I noticed it on my way to the music shop and had a quick look at what was on offer. It looks promising'

'Do you think we might give it a try?'

'So soon after the dance at the Wool Exchange? Mr Watson, I'm swept off my feet, but yes, I think we should.'

'Okay, I'll phone them, but I don't know what our families are going to make of all this dating and socialising, especially after all the talk there's been lately about black sheep.'

'You'll get used to it in time, Paul. I did.'

THE END